"I've been miserable without you," Alex murmured

Need, Serena thought. She could hear it in his gravelly voice, see it in the darkening storm of his eyes. The same need was thrumming through her body like a live wire, hot and dangerous. "I almost believe you mean that," she answered shakily.

"Believe it. I couldn't sleep for thinking of you. I couldn't work for wanting you." He pulled her closer in his arms. "If you're trying to drive me crazy, Serena, you're succeeding admirably."

"Show me," she urged, tilting her face up to his. "Show me how crazy I make you...."

JoAnn Ross had a soft spot for her character Alex Bedare, the sexy diplomat in *Magic in the Night*. So naturally she created a sequel around him, tossing in the lucky penny for good measure. The result? The delightfully funny and sensuous *Playing for Keeps*.

Believing that good things come in threes, JoAnn has written a third book to complete this heartwarming trilogy. *Tempting Fate*, to be published in May 1987, will follow the trials and tribulations of lovable Donovan Kincaid and his former flame, Brooke Stirling. Enjoy!

Books by JoAnn Ross

HARLEQUIN TEMPTATION
115–A HERO AT HEART
126–MAGIC IN THE NIGHT

HARLEQUIN INTRIGUE
27–RISKY PLEASURE
36–BAIT AND SWITCH

Playing for Keeps

JoANN ROSS

Harlequin Books

TORONTO • NEW YORK • LONDON
AMSTERDAM • PARIS • SYDNEY • HAMBURG
STOCKHOLM • ATHENS • TOKYO • MILAN

Published January 1987

ISBN 0-373-25237-4

1

IT WAS A RASH ACT, born of desperation. Later, she would remind herself that such precipitous behavior was bound to bring unforeseen results. But at this very moment, perched precariously on the rickety trellis, Serena Lawrence knew only that she had no choice.

Serena. Her very name suggested peace, tranquillity. It invited thoughts of gentle trade winds, fragrant, flower-dotted meadows, snow-covered hillocks. It was a name that fit her perfectly, which is why, under ordinary circumstances, she would have never stooped to scaling the ivy-covered brick wall under the cover of darkness, like a common cat burglar.

The party Serena was intent on crashing was, even to the most discriminating standards, a smashing success. The yard, illuminated with softly glowing lanterns, was abloom— purple bougainvillea blossoms competed with orange cape honeysuckle for claim to the most colorful, while creamy hibiscus added quiet sophistication to the displays of riotous colors. The pungent aroma of creeping rosemary filled the night air, mingling pleasantly with the heady Oriental scents of expensive perfumes.

The buffet table, exquisitely draped with snowy white Irish linen, groaned with a vast assortment of dishes, which were beautifully presented with the formality of a still life. The inevitable goat cheese—Californian, in honor of the occasion—resided on a bed of crisp, dark-green spinach leaves. There were tiny circlets of smoked eel on brioche, small squares of dark-pink salmon dabbed with glossy black caviar and peppery chopped chicken livers with colorful celery and carrots lavishly spread on circles of toasted Italian bread. At the far end of the table were sweet temptations—puff pastry wrapped around a cognac-flavored pastry cream and a hazelnut torte, the meringue layers sandwiched together with chocolate butter cream and topped with chocolate curls.

The estate bottled champagne flowed freely, the guests' crystal tulip glasses continually replenished by tanned young men clad in dark formal wear. The complex strains of baroque music, performed by a string quartet, accompanied the steady drone of conversation.

Yes, Serena considered, drinking in the exquisite scene, it was a most successful party. After scaling the forbidding wall, she had remained hidden in the shadows, surreptitiously observing the guests. Despite the importance of her mission, her eyes were continually drawn toward a single man. In his middle to late thirties, his dark eyes reminded her of obsidian, but without the flinty hardness. His face was lean—all planes and hollows—which, were it not for the brilliant smile that flashed regularly under the black mustache, might have made him appear harsh. He was tall, distinguished, with a great presence, yet Serena sensed in him a hint of the mystic.

She watched as several victims, male and female alike, fell under the spell of that dazzling smile. The fact that he was obviously foreign only added to his mystique, conjuring up fanciful visions of romantic Arabian nights. She found herself unwillingly intrigued.

Forging his way through the crowd of expensively attired individuals to the far fringes of the lawn, the man remained unaware of Serena's secret scrutiny as he mentally tallied the evening's haul. It had been a successful evening, all things considered. In exchange for a few hours' conversation, he had managed to pluck the party goers for several thousand dollars. The total figure might even end up in six figures. Believing himself to be all alone, he lifted the glass of champagne

he had been nursing all evening in a self-congratulatory salute.

Serena had observed him edging away from the throng of
guests and had decided that this man could possibly offer a
solution to her dilemma.

"You're very good," she said as he approached her hiding
spot.

At the unexpected voice, the man nearly dropped his glass.
He moved nearer to the veritable jungle of tropical plants that
took up this corner of the yard. "Who are you? Where are
you?"

"Right here. I've been watching you work." As Serena
emerged from behind a banana palm, her face struck a chord
of recognition in him. One he couldn't quite place.

Her slim black jeans and scarlet blouse gave evidence to the
fact that, whoever she was, this lissome young lady was a
gate-crasher. Her attire, while attractively emphasizing her
feminine attributes, was definitely unsuitable for such a formal affair. He decided that she was probably a college student.

"How long have you been hiding in the shrubbery?"

"Long enough to determine that you've got about the
smoothest touch I've ever seen. Most of those matrons didn't
even realize you were picking their pockets." Her lips quirked
in a hint of a smile when he opened his mouth to defend himself. "And those who did seem perfectly happy with the arrangement."

Serena's cool gray eyes moved from the top of his black
head down to his highly polished dress shoes. "Of course, it
probably doesn't hurt in your work to look a little like Omar
Sharif."

The masculine pleasure such words might normally arouse
was overshadowed by his concern over her unexpected appearance. Besides, Alexander Bedare reminded himself—al-

beit reluctantly in this case—students were off-limits, no matter how enticing.

"What are you doing here?"

She crossed her arms and leaned back against a tree. "Don't I look as if I belong in such exalted company?"

The funny thing about it, he considered, was that she did. Despite her casual attire, the jeans were not the type to come off the rack of a local discount store. And the crimson blouse was silk. However, her clothes were not what gave her away. She possessed an unmistakable aura of quality that no amount of money could buy. Something several of the guests at the party tonight would never attain. Her manner, as she eyed him dispassionately, was oddly regal.

Even so, Alex had the feeling her cool reserve was merely a matter of protective coloring, designed to conceal a more passionate nature. Perhaps it was wishful thinking on his part that she possessed fire under that icy exterior, but experience had taught him to trust his instincts. And when it came to the feminine sex, Alex's instincts were seldom mistaken.

The soft drone of party conversation faded into the distance as Serena found herself enthralled by the lambent flame suddenly gleaming in those hooded dark eyes. She was vaguely aware of a harp strumming in the background, a muted laugh, the clink of crystal.

Bingo. Alex's instincts were vindicated as her gray eyes momentarily widened before darkening to polished pewter. So there *was* warmth there, after all. Interesting. Ignoring the automatic sexual pull, he turned his mind to why she had crashed the party. He considered the unpleasant fact that she could be part of a radical college protest group, here to stage a demonstration. There had been rumors of such a proposed act floating around the campus all week.

"How do you feel about whales?" he asked.

Serena blinked, distracted by his abrupt conversational maneuver. "Wales? Having never been there, I've no idea. I suppose if I were pushed to come up with an impression I'd say wet and cold. With moors right out of a Brontë novel."

"Not *Wales*. Whales. The mammal."

She shrugged her shoulders. "I suppose they're okay. I wouldn't want one for a pet, it'd never fit in my bathtub, but I'm not in favor of fishing fleets killing them, either."

"So you're not a member of Greenpeace? Or one of those other environmental groups?"

"No, I'm not. Are you?"

"No."

Serena was becoming confused. "Then why did you ask?"

Determined to discern the reason for her inauspicious appearance, Alex didn't immediately respond to her question. "How do you feel about nuclear war?"

She was staring at him now. "I'm against it, of course. Isn't everyone?"

"Some people feel more strongly than others."

Serena studied him thoughtfully. The deep lines fanning out from his dark eyes indicated that this was a man who laughed easily. And often. But there was something else there as well. She could recognize a core of pure steel, since she possessed a fair amount of that personality trait herself. He was obviously irritated by her presence, a fact that after a long, wearisome day did nothing for her own mood.

"Is this your usual cocktail-party patter? You'll excuse me if I fail to understand how you charm the dollars out of all those pockets. Personally, I don't think I'd chip in two cents."

Something flashed in his eyes. It could have been amusement or aggravation. Whatever, it was gone before Serena could detect its source.

"What makes you think I've been trying to charm you?"

"I think it's probably standard operating procedure," she returned. "Don't forget, I've seen you in action."

He nodded. "So you have. But you're off the hook; I've never found protestors to be a very good source of funds. For some strange reason, they never seem willing to put their money behind their words."

Serena was momentarily dumbfounded. "You think I'm a protestor?"

His dark eyes narrowed suspiciously. "Aren't you here for some sort of demonstration?"

It had taken every bit of his lobbying skills to coax the alumni into increasing their donations to the college, but Alex had garnered a significant number of pledges. He wasn't going to allow this woman to ruin what he'd worked so hard to accomplish here tonight. It didn't matter that she was undeniably appealing. The minute she opened her mouth, he was going to drag her out the back gate.

Serena's laughter bubbled forth, a silvery, musical sound worlds away from any strident, slogan-chanting protestor he'd ever heard. Her amusement moved to her eyes, brightening them to a brilliant sterling.

"Do you know," she said a little breathlessly, "that's the nicest compliment anyone has ever paid me."

"Compliment?" It was his turn to be confused.

"I've been called the 'Ice Princess' for so long the idea that anyone would take me for a campus radical is absolutely delicious."

Comprehension dawned. "You're Serena Lawrence."

Even as she confirmed his words with a nod, Alex couldn't quite accept the idea that this slender young woman was the same individual who had taken the tennis world by storm when she was fourteen years old. Serena Lawrence had risen out of the clay tennis courts onto the covers of both sports and fan magazines like a Botticelli Venus. It had been impossible to pass a newsstand without seeing those wide gray eyes looking back at you, he remembered. She had been pretty, graceful and, before that summer was over, famous.

He did some rapid mental calculations, putting her at twenty-eight. Even granting her the benefit of the muted landscape lighting, she didn't look a day over twenty-one.

She put her hand on his sleeve. "Would you do me a favor and not spread it around that I'm here? I'm really not in any mood to be in the spotlight tonight. Besides, as you've no doubt noticed, I'm not dressed for such an august affair."

He glanced down at the hand resting lightly on his arm. Her fingers were long and slender, the short, efficient nails unpolished. It crossed his mind that it was an extremely graceful hand for one so strong. Alex knew Serena Lawrence's deceptive strength; he had marveled at it two years ago watching her sweep the French Open, then Wimbledon.

The tragic car accident that had taken the life of her mixed-doubles partner and onetime fiancé a week before the U.S. Open had left her seriously injured. He recalled reading that Serena was attempting a comeback. His eyes slid to her right arm.

"It still won't tan," Serena said easily as she followed his gaze to the jagged white scar that twisted around her forearm, ending at the elbow. "But at least it doesn't look like steak tartar any longer."

Alex was infused with embarrassment. It was not often that he was caught being totally tactless. "I'm sorry. That wasn't very polite of me."

She forced a careless shrug. "There's no need to apologize. It's a common enough reaction."

"I suppose it gets old." When she looked up at him questioningly, he elaborated. "The fact that total strangers know everything about you."

Those lovely eyes, which had fascinated him from the beginning, frosted. "No one knows *everything* about me," she snapped. "It may interest you to know that, media attention aside, I'm a very private person."

There it was again. That enticing spark of passion. Alex wondered if Serena ever allowed it free rein. He couldn't help being intrigued by the possibility.

"I can understand your desire for privacy," he drawled. "But don't you think that wearing jeans to a formal fund-raising party is bound to attract a scintilla of attention?"

As Serena felt her blood begin to boil, she was astonished by the way this man had gotten under her skin. She had spent years subduing her fiery temper; she could not allow him to undo a lifetime of effort. Especially not now, when her entire future was at stake.

Her frustrated sigh ruffled her pale-blond bangs. "Look, whoever you are, I've enjoyed our little chat immensely, but it just so happens that I've had a rotten day. My alarm clock decided to pick this particular morning to conk out, causing me to oversleep. In a hurry to dress, once I did wake up, I spilled coffee on my only clean dress and was forced to wear this outfit you seem to find so distasteful."

She drew a deep breath before continuing. "Then, on the way to the airport, the taxi blew a tire. Luckily, no one was hurt, but I did miss my plane and had to make my way west on a flying cattle car that must have stopped at every city with a population of five hundred or more from Durham, North Carolina, to LAX. My bags were taken off somewhere—they think El Paso, but no one knows for certain—so I arrived in Los Angeles with only my purse, which contained eighteen dollars, which wasn't enough to pay the cab driver who brought me here to Claremont. Fortunately, he believed I was good for it and settled for the eighteen dollars plus an autograph. I've promised to mail him the rest, plus a generous tip."

"You have had a bad day." Alex wondered how she managed to look so good after such a wearying experience. "Is that where you're from? North Carolina?" Odd that he couldn't detect an accent; his ear was usually attuned to such things.

"I've lived there the past few years," she answered in an offhand way. "And believe me, as bad as that was, it gets even worse. I finally arrived in town, fourteen hours after I began this trek, to discover that my house key is in that suitcase stranded somewhere in the bleak outback of west Texas."

Serena's eyes swept his face as if she were questioning something. She apparently made a decision as she nodded to herself. "So, this is where you come in."

"You want me to break into your house?"

"No. I want you to be a nice, helpful man and go ask Donovan Kincaid for his key."

Alex was suddenly very still. His gaze moved from Serena to scan the sea of tuxedo-clad men until he came to Donovan Kincaid. He knew the man, of course. Not only were they both lecturing at the same college, they were also next-door neighbors. But Donovan had never offered the information that he was on such friendly terms with the former sweetheart of professional tennis.

He returned his attention to Serena. "Donovan's a lucky man."

"I'm the lucky one," Serena said simply.

As he forged his way through the guests crowding the backyard of the distinguished alumnus, Alex spotted Donovan and a tall, leggy redhead edging their way toward the back gate. He reached them just as they were prepared to leave the yard.

"Donovan, I need to talk with you."

Donovan Kincaid appeared understandably disconcerted by his neighbor's untimely appearance. "Sure, Alex. Some other time, okay? How about a game of tennis tomorrow afternoon after my three o'clock seminar?"

"Sounds great," Alex agreed. "But another one of your tennis partners has just arrived in town." At Donovan's questioning look, Alex jerked his head in the direction of the palm tree.

"I'll be damned," Donovan murmured.

Alex said a mental prayer that the threesome would choose to settle things quietly, without upsetting the party. He could practically see all those alumni checks sprouting wings and flying away into the night sky. As his attention focused on Donovan's companion more closely, Alex recognized her to be Dr. Paula Taylor, from the biology department.

It was no wonder he hadn't made the connection more quickly—the clinging red-knit dress was a far cry from the white lab coat she usually wore. And the unabashedly romantic floral scent wafting from her creamy skin was definitely not formaldehyde. L'Air du Temps, he determined as he waited for Donovan's response. Alex had bought enough of the intensely feminine perfume for women over the years to recognize it immediately.

"Would you be a sport and keep Paula company for a minute?" Donovan asked. "I'd better see what's up." He slanted a quick, apologetic smile Paula Taylor's way. "This won't take long."

Although Alex could tell that the lovely Dr. Taylor was less than pleased with the sudden appearance of a potential rival in their midst, she managed to return Donovan's smile with a stiff one of her own. Neither she nor Alex were inclined toward conversation as they watched the little drama being played out in the far corner of the yard.

Serena's smile broke free, stunning in its wattage as she flung her arms around Donovan's neck. They exchanged a long embrace.

"You look terrific." Loving lights gleamed in Donovan's green eyes as they skimmed over her upturned face.

She tossed the compliment off. "Thanks. But look at you! You look even more terrific. You should wear a tux all the time. It makes you appear almost distinguished."

Her eyes took a quick tour of the tall, lanky man, loving what she saw. Thank God, after all that had changed in her life, Donovan had remained exactly the same. His nut-brown hair was boyishly tousled, his jacket rumpled as if he had slept in it, his black tie disarmingly askew. On his feet, instead of the obligatory dress shoes, he was wearing a pair of sneakers.

"How's the arm?" He ran his index finger tenderly down the scar.

"Better. But I'll know a lot more in a few weeks."

"I read about the charity tournament. I was hoping you'd deign to visit me while you were in the valley." His tone held just the faintest tinge of censure.

Serena reached up to place her palm tenderly against his bearded cheek. "How could I not?" she asked softly.

"I suppose the same way you refused to allow me to visit you in the clinic," Donovan returned gruffly.

Watching from across the yard, Alex was admittedly curious at the intimate scene taking place. Despite the more than obvious love between Serena Lawrence and Donovan Kincaid, something seemed not quite right. Serena appeared momentarily stricken as she dropped her hand to her side.

"I thought I'd explained all that." Her expression was intense as she strived to make Donovan understand. "My rehabilitation was something I had to do by myself. If you'd been there, my sweet, loving Donovan, I wouldn't have been strong enough to pull it off."

"I know you believe that, but you're dead wrong on this one," he protested. He took her hand in his, linking their fingers together. "Love doesn't have to make you weak."

Serena shook her head in mute disagreement. "I had to do this myself."

Donovan expelled a resigned sigh. He had never met an individual as intransigent as Serena Lawrence. Or as ultimately vulnerable, whether she would admit it or not.

"Let's not rehash old grievances," he suggested with a pacifying grin. "It's enough that you're finally here. I can't wait to hear your plans." He slanted a glance across the yard. "I just have one slight little problem to clear up."

Serena's eyes followed his to Paula Taylor. "Don't let me interfere with your plans for the evening. I'd be lousy company tonight, anyway. All I want to do is to go home, take a hot bath and go to bed."

Donovan appeared uncertain. "Are you sure you don't mind?"

Serena went up on her toes and planted a quick kiss on his cheek. "Positive." She pushed him lightly away. "Just let me have the key to the house and I'll be out of here."

Donovan dug into a pocket of his slacks and came up empty. Serena, familiar with the routine, waited patiently as he searched the other pocket. Wrinkles furrowed his brow as he moved to the jacket pockets, finally extracting a key ring fashioned from a twisted piece of copper wire. He took off a single key and handed it to her.

"I'll see you in the morning," he said. Before leaving, Donovan folded her in his arms. "God, it's good to see you," he murmured against her silky hair.

"You've no idea how wonderful it is to be home." Serena's smile wobbled only slightly as she watched him walk away.

"Thanks for keeping Paula company," Donovan said to Alex as he returned to the avidly watching twosome.

Alex—who had been called a rake, a Casanova, a womanizer of the worst ilk—stared in stunned amazement as Donovan Kincaid proceeded to put his arm around Dr. Paula Taylor's lithe waist and lead the sexy biology professor through the gate.

"I'm sorry about that," he said as soon as he returned to Serena.

She appeared not to have heard him. Instead she kissed the brass key. "Do you have any idea what this is?" she asked without giving him time to answer. "This is a bath. A hot, delicious bath filled to the brim with frothy, fragrant bubbles. This is a bed. A wonderful water bed that doesn't sag from broken springs or feel like a slab of granite. This is a kitchen, the shelves stocked with blissful herbal teas." She sighed happily. "This is heaven."

She turned, headed back through the dense foliage. "Well, thanks again. I really do appreciate your help."

Although Alex didn't know why, he wasn't prepared to let her get away. Not quite yet. "The gate's in the other direction."

"I know. But I'd have to cross the yard in front of all those people to get there," Serena answered over her shoulder. "Don't worry, the trellis is a lot sturdier than it looks."

"At least let me walk you home."

"Don't worry about me, I'll be fine. Donovan's house isn't that far away and as you've undoubtedly discovered, Claremont is a very friendly town."

Alex considered Drs. Taylor and Kincaid and silently agreed. The two of them had certainly appeared friendly enough. But where, exactly, did that leave Serena Lawrence? And what was it about the woman that allowed her to take things so calmly? He had already decided that she was not nearly as cool as her reputation suggested.

"I'm ready to leave," he said. "Since I'm headed the same way, we may as well keep each other company."

"You live near Donovan?"

"Next door." He cupped her elbow in his palm to give her a boost up the trellis. "Small world, isn't it?"

"Indeed," Serena murmured.

She didn't look back as she scaled the wall; the rickety ivy-covered trellis demanded all her attention. It swayed precariously, and for a fleeting moment when the creaking became particularly ominous, Serena was afraid that she was going to fall onto her well-publicized backside. Wouldn't that make a terrific photo for the supermarket tabloids, she considered with a wry grin. The dark-green leaves, moistened by the night air, were slippery, making the task even more difficult.

Finally, with a sigh of satisfaction, she breached the wall, swinging her legs over the top. Alex, having opted for the gate, was waiting for her. His long fingers easily spanned her waist as he helped her down, the warmth they created doing nothing to instill calm.

She tried to repress the slight, unexpected shiver his touch generated, but Alex's dark eyes were too observant. Serena didn't argue as he slipped out of his jacket and placed it over her shoulders. It was preferable to let him believe she was chilled from the night air rather than to permit him to discern her true feelings.

Serena had watched him work the crowd with the skilled performance of a faith healer. He was too smooth for comfort. She had the feeling that if those ebony eyes ever looked at her the way they had looked at Mildred Hemming Wright, class of '35, he wouldn't be after a mere check. What was even more disconcerting was her intuition that she would not be able to refuse him with any more success than the blue-haired Mrs. Wright.

Serena found the sparks he had ignited in her undeniably distracting. Even during those long, agonizing months of rehabilitative therapy, when her mood had swung back and forth between discouragement and anger, she had never allowed her tumultuous emotions to surface. Instead, she had concentrated on conquering the pain and recovering her strength as her late father would have wished.

William Lawrence, Serena's father, had been one of Great Britain's premier tennis stars, one of the few Englishmen able to compete with the steady stream of Australian and American players who began to dominate the game after World War Two. He had played with an icy precision, a style he drilled into his daughter from the time he had first put a racket in her hand on her fifth birthday.

Despite her natural talent, William had been aghast to learn that Serena had inherited her mother's tempestuous temperament. That unwelcome discovery had prompted first father, then later daughter, to wage a continual battle against nature. A battle Serena was accustomed to winning. That was the reason this man's ability to create such bursts of emotion within her was an unwelcome surprise.

"Have you known Donovan long?" Serena inquired as they walked.

The moon was creeping through the trees lining the sidewalk, tangling in their branches, silvering the leaves. The streaming moon dust made her sleek blond curtain of hair shine like polished silk and Alex had to fight the urge to touch it, to see if it felt as soft as it looked.

"Since September," he answered, forcing his mind back to her question. "This is my first year here."

She glanced over at him. "This isn't your usual line of work, is it?"

He lifted a dark brow. "Is it that obvious? You haven't even seen me lecture."

"It's not that. I just don't know many academicians who can afford a custom-tailored dinner jacket."

Alex was tempted to ask exactly how many academicians, besides Donovan Kincaid, Serena was acquainted with but reluctantly decided that it was none of his business.

"You've a good eye," he said instead.

"And you've a knack for dodging questions," Serena returned silkily. "What's your field?"

"International relations."

She nodded knowingly. "That explains it."

"Explains what?"

A triumphant gleam lit her moon-silvered eyes. "You're obviously a career diplomat."

Alex glanced down at his stiffly pleated shirtfront. "I hadn't realized my scarlet D was showing."

Serena ticked the clues off on her fingertips. "Number one, your clothes. Very few men manage to appear comfortable in a tuxedo. You, however, look as if you exited the womb wearing a dinner jacket.

"Two, you're about as smooth a fund-raiser as I've ever watched in action. You cleaned up back there, deftly avoiding any controversial topics. And three, you've an annoying habit of never giving a direct answer."

She stopped suddenly to look up at him. "I just realized I don't even know your name."

There had been a reason for that, Alex acknowledged inwardly. For a brief, enjoyable time he had been anonymous. Just another man meeting a pretty woman at a party.

"That's right," he agreed. "You don't. Are you hungry?"

He was doing it again, Serena realized, stifling her burst of irritation. But if there was one thing the past two years had taught her, it was patience.

"I ate on the plane, Mr . . ."

Alex ignored the pointed hint. "How about dessert?" he asked as they passed an ice-cream parlor on the main street of the village. "I could go for some butter pecan myself."

"Make mine vanilla," Serena said with a sigh, giving up for the time being.

They still had a few more blocks to go before they arrived at Donovan's house. She was determined that by the time she reached his wide front porch, she would have learned something about Donovan's next-door neighbor. Not that she was personally interested in the man; it was simply that his reticence had piqued her curiosity. That's all it was, Serena assured herself firmly. That's all she would allow it to be.

2

As THE COLLEGE STUDENT WORKING behind the counter dished up their ice-cream cones, Serena decided that her companion's unwillingness to divulge his identity only added to the aura of mystique she had sensed the moment she had first seen him.

After finally arriving at Donovan's house earlier this evening, Serena had discovered a note on his front door, left for someone named Paula. The note had claimed a slight emergency with yet another woman named Gloria and suggested they meet at the party. Three years ago, when she had been at the top of her game, Donovan had taken her to dinner at the home of the retired neurosurgeon and distinguished Smiley College alumnus. The physician, a highly ranked amateur player, had been thrilled to meet Serena Lawrence. Her presence had resulted in a generous check being donated toward Donovan's ongoing primate studies.

Once she had managed to sneak into the backyard this evening, Serena had scanned the crowd, searching for Donovan. But her eyes had returned time and time again to the tall, intriguing man with the ebony eyes and disturbingly sensual mouth.

The one thing Serena found difficult to fathom was the fact that this man and Donovan were friends. As dearly as she loved him, Serena could not deny that Donovan Kincaid was the quintessential absentminded professor. He was unworldly, completely disinterested in appearances—she had witnessed him wearing mismatched socks on more than one occasion—and his color combinations could awaken the dead. He had absolutely no sense of time; when engrossed in a particularly intriguing research project he had been known to disappear for hours, often days, into his laboratory.

While Donovan's brilliance more than made up for his flaws, Serena could not envision him having anything in common with his cosmopolitan neighbor. Yet as she had watched the brief discussion between the two men, that had seemed to be the case. Before she could dwell on the mystery any longer, Alex handed her a sugar cone.

"Thank you." She licked the rich ice cream. "Mmm, this was a good idea. It's delicious."

"I would have figured you for something a bit more adventurous than vanilla," he said as they left the ice-cream shop. Bathed in moonlight, the small but charming little village on the outskirts of the campus proper seemed a very long way from the sprawling city of Los Angeles. In reality, it was a mere thirty-five miles.

Serena thought she detected a question in his tone and shrugged. "I've had enough adventure the past few years to last a lifetime."

"I can understand how you might feel that way," Alex answered.

"I doubt that," she snapped. Damn. She had done it again. Her loss of control had been fleeting, but she couldn't deny it had happened. If only he hadn't sounded so blasted sympathetic.

If there was one thing Serena hated worse than losing a match or her temper, it was receiving unsolicited pity from strangers. During those weeks she had been confined to the hospital after the accident, the letters and cards had flooded in by the thousands. In the beginning she had been heartened by the outpouring of support and concern. But she was to discover that people were not willing to let her put the incident behind her and get on with her life.

She grew weary of the continual stream of articles depicting her valiant struggle to survive the tragedy that had taken Brett Nelson's life. Their engagement, born of the closeness of two teenagers thrown together continually on the tour, had ended amiably, allowing them to remain friends. But the public, who had watched the young romance flourish, preferred to believe the cool, composed Serena Lawrence and the volatile Brett Nelson were still wildly in love and needed only to work out their differences before treating the world to a storybook wedding.

Now, with Brett gone, the stories ranged from unanimously depressing predictions about the future of her career to out-and-out fabrications printed in supermarket tabloids. One article had proclaimed that Serena was carrying Brett's love child. Another seconded that supposition while announcing that they had been secretly married the week of the French Open. The most outrageous story of all was the allegation that Serena regularly conversed with Brett's ghost.

If she had thought the passage of time would at least put a stop to the ridiculous claim about her pregnancy, Serena was to be sadly mistaken. The tabloids, not willing to confess that they had made a grievous error, took a new tack, declaring that, unable to withstand the constant reminder of her tragically lost love, Serena had obtained a secret abortion. That story had generated a new flood of mail, most of it negative. She had been surprised when a handful of letters arrived from women all over the world, each claiming to be the mother of Brett's child. Serena had immediately contacted Brett's family to warn them about the existence of these fanciful individuals, only to learn that several paternity suits had already been filed against Brett's estate.

Having practically grown up with Brett on the tour, Serena knew him to be a man of honor. Although he was admittedly reckless, he would never have behaved so irresponsibly as to turn his back on his own child. While his

death had caused her enormous grief, the fact that these un-
balanced women continued to damage his good name and his
family's peace was additionally depressing. Serena sighed
now, just thinking about it.

Alex glanced down at her curiously. Her mouth was drawn
in a grim, taut line and her eyes were shadowed with obvious distress. After his own experience, he understood her
frustration with the publicity surrounding both her accident
and her attempted comeback.

"You know, while you've had it rough, you're not the first
person in the world to get a raw deal," he said.

Something in his tone alerted Serena. Finishing her cone,
she tossed her napkin into a waste bin on the corner and
turned to look up at him.

"I'm sorry I bit your head off. I'm really never tempera-
mental. As I said, I've had a rotten day. But that's no excuse."

Her throaty voice was soft, her tone conciliatory. What the
hell, Alex considered fatalistically, how could he expect Serena to realize that they had far more in common than she
could ever suspect? He hadn't even told her his name.

His engaging smile granted absolution. "Don't worry
about it."

She returned the smile with a slightly hesitant one of her
own and the antagonism faded away as quickly as it had
flared. They crossed Harvard Avenue in companionable silence.

As they approached Donovan's house, Serena experienced a flood of relief. While it wasn't exactly home, it was
the nearest thing she had to one. That feeling slowly gave way
to curiosity as she studied the Edwardian house in more detail, spotting things she had been too disconcerted to notice
earlier.

The blue shake siding had been painted. Scarlet and white
petunias cascaded over clay pots lining the generous railing

on his front porch. The creaky old porch swing not only boasted new blue-and-white striped pillows, but a matching awning as well. Donovan had never displayed any interest in his surroundings; he had always directed all his energies toward his work. In that respect, he and Serena were soul mates.

The fact that Donovan had gone to this much trouble to fix up the house he had inherited so many years ago suggested that he was settling down. While a life in some nice, quiet college town wasn't Serena's idea of nirvana, she honestly hoped that he would be happy.

"He's painted it," she murmured, more to herself than to Alex.

"I wouldn't know. It was this color when I arrived in town."

Her eyes scanned the two-story house with its charming white cupolas. "It used to be a lot more weathered."

"Sounds as if you spend a lot of time here," he said conversationally. In truth, Alex was digging for information. He still hadn't unraveled Serena Lawrence's relationship with his neighbor.

"As a former diplomat, you should be able to do a great deal better than that," she said as they made their way up the wide steps to the porch. He had even nailed down that loose board, Serena noted absently. "Although I have no idea why you want to know how often I visit my brother, why don't you come right out and ask?"

Alex's initial embarrassment over being caught in less than subtle behavior disintegrated as her words sank in. "Brother?"

Serena nodded. "Brother," she agreed. "Stepbrother, if you want to get technical. But surely you knew..." Her voice trailed off. "Oh, my God, did you honestly believe that I'd stand there with a big grin on my face while the man I loved waltzed off with some curvaceous redhead?"

"I thought that was a little surprising," Alex admitted. "But then I decided that you must be a terrific sport."

"I'm not," Serena stated firmly as she took the key from the pocket of her jeans and went to unlock the heavy oak front door.

Knowing her absentminded brother as well as she did, Serena was not surprised to discover Donovan had failed to lock it in the first place. She could have saved herself a great deal of time and effort if she had simply tried the door earlier.

"Actually," she said, continuing the conversation, "I'm one of the worst sports around."

"I certainly wouldn't have guessed that by the way you played. I don't remember seeing you ever react to a mishit or contest a call."

Serena shrugged. "I discovered early in life that if I allowed my emotions free rein while playing, they messed up my game." When she entered the house without saying goodbye, Alex took her behavior as an invitation to follow.

"So the Ice Princess was born."

"That's about it. Can I get you something to drink?"

Despite the fact that he made her a little uncomfortable, good manners had been instilled into Serena at an early age. She felt she owed him something for his willingness to help, even if the act had proven ultimately unnecessary. Besides, she still hadn't learned a thing about her mystery guest's identity.

"Scotch would be great," he agreed. "I never have developed a taste for champagne, despite the fact that it always seems to show up at functions like tonight's."

"One Scotch coming right up." Serena turned toward the kitchen, where she knew Donovan kept his well-hoarded stash of liquor.

"Why don't you let me get the drinks?" Alex suggested. "You must be suffering from jet lag about now."

"You've got yourself a deal." She kicked off her running shoes and, after removing a stack of textbooks and scientific journals from the cushions of the couch, settled down with a deep sigh.

"What would you like?"

"A glass of juice would be nice. Whatever you find in the refrigerator will do. By the way, Donovan keeps the good stuff hidden away underneath the kitchen sink."

That was news to him. Alex wondered if the lovely Dr. Taylor would have been treated to the premium liquor if things had worked out differently tonight, and decided that she would. Not that Alex wouldn't have behaved in precisely the same way, had he been in Donovan's shoes. Fortunately, Alex was not dependent on his salary at the college for survival. He possessed more than ample funds for life's small pleasures.

"I'd feel guilty raiding his cache."

Serena had risen from the couch and was rifling through a stack of record albums. "Don't worry about it. Besides, between the both of us, I think we can afford to pitch in and buy him a replacement bottle, don't you?"

"It may prove a sacrifice, but I can probably spare a few of the hard-earned dollars the college is paying me," Alex agreed before leaving the room to retrieve their drinks.

When he returned, the unmistakable sounds of Gilbert and Sullivan were emanating from the stereo speakers and Serena was stretched out on the couch, her eyes closed, her lashes a dark fringe against her cheeks. Her toenails were polished a glistening pink in a display of feminine vanity that surprised him. From what he could tell, Serena eschewed makeup altogether. Her blond hair was short and sleek, curving just under her chin. The rosy tint of her lips owed nothing to cosmetics, nor did her lush dark lashes. Natural was the word that came immediately to mind.

Unable to discern whether or not she had fallen asleep, Alex stood looking down at her, a glass in each hand. Seeming to sense his appearance, Serena opened her eyes.

"Sorry about that," she said as she sat up. "I have this nasty habit of falling asleep at the drop of a hat." She swiveled her feet to the floor, making room for him to sit beside her.

"That's probably a necessity in your business." He handed her the glass.

"And yours as well, I would imagine." Serena took a sip of the tangy apple juice. "This is great, thank you."

"I had a hard time making up my mind which you'd want," he said. "Donovan seems to be quite a juice advocate. He had the refrigerator stocked with just about every kind imaginable."

"It's his monkeys. Well, actually, his apes," she corrected herself, remembering how the one thing that could rile her usually calm brother was the misnomer of his varied charges. "He buys fruit for them by the bushel and when it starts to go soft, he makes it into juice."

"Don't tell me they'd object to eating overripe fruit?" Alex asked incredulously.

Serena took another sip. "I don't think so, but Donovan has always spoiled them rotten. Heaven help us all if he ever becomes a father. If he brings his parenting technique home from the lab, my nieces and nephews will turn out to be little demons.

"Since we're going to be neighbors for the next few weeks, don't you think I should know your name?" she suggested, deftly changing the subject. While there was nothing strident in her soft tone, Alex understood it to be more command than request.

He carefully took a sip of the twelve-year-old Scotch. When he turned toward her, his dark eyes were unreadable. "My name is Alex. Alexander Bedare."

Serena tried to catch the gasp before it escaped her lips and failed. *And I accused this man of not being able to understand the pressures of an insensitive press,* she groaned inwardly.

Despite her preoccupation with her own problems over the past year, Serena had most certainly heard of Alexander Bedare. His father had been Egypt's minister of trade, his mother an economics professor at the American University in Cairo. When a radical terrorist faction assassinated the trade minister for increasing the nation's business dealings with the United States, scenes of the brutal shooting had dominated the airwaves before giving way to a military coup in Central America.

Alex, Serena remembered, had been assigned to the Egyptian embassy in Washington at the time. Ignoring threats made on his own life, he had gone to Cairo to arrange for his father's burial in the family crypt. As the world watched, Alexander Bedare paid his last respects to a man he had always loved and admired. Then he had returned to the United States with his American mother.

Serena recalled reading that Alex had stated the understandable need to take a respite from the world of international politics—the arena where his father had given his life—in order to try the academic life for a time. She was certain the article had not mentioned at which college Alex would be lecturing. Surely, even with her own problems, she would have noticed if the writer had named the school where Donovan was on staff.

"I believe I owe you an apology," she said quietly.

Alex merely moved his shoulders. "Don't worry about it. It's all over and done with. Besides, you've had a bad day."

"You know, that's becoming a very handy excuse." A light shone in her eyes. "How long do you think I can milk it?"

He chuckled. "Probably as long as you want. I've certainly used it enough times myself."

"Most men do," Serena acknowledged. "Bad day at the office, the embassy, or the classroom and all that." She held out her hand. "Want to shake and make up?"

"Now how can I refuse that?"

His fingers closed around the slender hand Serena offered. As a diplomat, Alex had experienced every conceivable handshake known to man and was a firm believer that the social act revealed a great deal about a person.

There were those who felt they had to prove immediately superiority by crushing your fingers while observing you carefully to see if you winced. On the opposite end of the scale were individuals who barely touched fingers. Alex had encountered politicians who utilized this method while campaigning to avoid being pulled into crowds. Women often just allowed their hands to slip into yours, expecting you to do all the work.

But there was nothing tentative about Serena's grip and while she did not pump his arm like a Washington lobbyist, she shook his hand with a firm, brisk motion. His thumb brushed against a row of calluses, something he was unaccustomed to feeling on a woman's palm.

Alex found himself looking forward to getting to know her better. Serena Lawrence was a tantalizing blend of strength and femininity; he had an overwhelming urge to strip away her icy armor, layer by intriguing layer, until he finally reached the passion he knew existed deep inside her. It wasn't going to be easy. She had obviously spent a lifetime developing that aura of cool restraint she was able to wrap around herself like a protective cloak. But if there was one thing Alex enjoyed, it was a challenge. And Serena definitely represented one of the more interesting, not to mention attractive, ones he had encountered in a very long time.

"Scotch as good as this deserves a toast," he said. His dark eyes swept over her face slowly, intimately. "And I know just the thing to drink to."

"I'll just bet you do," Serena responded, bracing herself for the proposition she felt coming her way.

Ignoring her dry tone, Alex smiled disarmingly as he lifted his glass toward her. "To Serena Lawrence's successful return to the tennis world."

His friendly expression momentarily beguiled her, causing Serena to drop her guard. "Thank you." She lifted her own glass as well, only to discover she had relaxed a moment too soon.

"And to our own little game as well," he tacked on with consummate smoothness.

Serena complimented herself on her ability to meet his liquid gaze levelly. "Our game?"

"Our game," he repeated. "The one we've begun here tonight." When he ran a finger down her cheek, his gentle touch seemed to scorch her skin.

Serena reminded herself that she had certainly handled her share of passes from men. There was nothing to worry about. She appeared unruffled as she lifted the glass of apple juice to her lips.

"I'm afraid you're mistaken."

Alex took her hand in his, encouraged when he found it to be as icy as her voice. She could lie with her words, but never her body. His dark, fathomless eyes locked on hers as he brushed his thumb enticingly over her knuckles.

"No," he corrected quietly, but firmly. "I'm not."

Serena sucked in a harsh breath as he lifted her hand to his lips. His black mustache feathered across the skin his fingers had warmed. Before she could recover from the assault to her senses created by that innocent touch, he flashed her a wicked grin and rose lazily to his feet.

"I'd better let you get some sleep. After all, you're going to need all your strength for the days ahead." His gleaming eyes assured Serena that he was not referring to her upcoming tennis match.

Alex was halfway to the door when he turned, eyeing her over his shoulder. "Oh, and Serena?"

She hadn't moved from the couch. "Yes?"

Again that dangerous, devastating smile. "May the best man—or woman—win."

With that sensual challenge lingering in the air between them, he turned on his heel and let himself out of Donovan's house. As he made his way across the expanse of dark-green ivy that took the place of a lawn between the two houses, Alex chuckled as he considered Serena's stunned expression.

The game was just beginning. A game he had every intention of winning. For the first time in over a year, Alex found himself looking forward to the future.

IF SHE HAD FOUND Alex Bedare dangerous last night, Serena knew she was in trouble when he ran by the house the following morning as she was sitting on the front porch swing. The man had been positively handsome in formal dress; in a pair of faded blue gym shorts and running shoes he was magnificent. She drew in an involuntary breath at the sight of his dark chest glistening with a sheen of perspiration.

Alex spotted Serena the moment he turned the corner. She had appropriated a robe from her brother's closet and as he neared the front porch, Alex was surprised by her appearance. On the tennis court Serena Lawrence had dominated play so strongly that she had appeared larger than life. In person, swathed in those voluminous folds of maroon material, she appeared almost frail. A pair of Donovan's bulky ski socks climbed up her legs like fuzzy black and red caterpillars. She held a cup of coffee in her hand.

He stopped in front of her. "Good morning."

"Good morning." She was pleased that her casual tone failed to reveal the shock he had imparted to her senses.

Reluctant to allow his body to cool down too rapidly, he did a few deep knee bends. "How did you sleep?"

Serena's eyes were unwillingly drawn to Alex's hard, elon gated thigh muscles. "Like a rock," she lied.

In truth, she had tossed and turned, her mind conjuring up unwelcome images of her brother's next-door neighbor. By the time the pale fingers of dawn had come creeping over the horizon, Serena had attributed her atypical behavior to ex haustion, jet lag and stress over her upcoming match—her first in more than two years.

"Good." His gaze scanned her face. Despite the faint shad ows under them, her gray eyes were clear, her complexion free of makeup in the soft early-morning light. "California must agree with you. You're the loveliest woman I've seen since moving to the state."

She forced a casual tone. "Then you must not have been paying proper attention. California is overrun with far more attractive women."

"Really?"

"Really. Ask the Beach Boys if you won't take my word for it."

"I suppose I've been too busy working to notice."

Fat chance of that, Serena considered. She murmured a soft sound that could have been agreement, argument or sheer disgust.

"Do you have any more of that coffee?" he asked sud denly. "I ran out yesterday and never made it to the store."

Despite the proximity of their houses, Serena had no in tention of becoming too close to Donovan's neighbor. She had to keep her mind on tennis, where it belonged. She couldn't allow distractions at this time in her life. And Alex was, without a doubt, the most unsettling distraction she had ever run up against.

"Don't you have a class?"

"It's Friday. Classes don't begin for another hour."

"Oh. Well, I suppose I can offer you a cup," she agreed without enthusiasm.

"That's what I love about this state," Alex answered cheerfully. "While I'd always heard rumors about western hospitality, it's terrific to see it in action. Let me grab a shirt from next door and I'll be right back."

Serena went into the house to pour Alex's coffee, refilling her own cup. She was debating changing into her blouse and jeans from last night when a glance out the kitchen window showed him already on the way back across the ivy front yard. The one thing she wasn't going to risk was undressing with this man anywhere in proximity. Besides, she decided, glancing down at the expanse of maroon, Donovan's robe covered everything.

She returned to the porch to be joined by Alex as he took the steps two at a time. "You are an angel," he proclaimed, taking the cup she offered.

"It's only a cup of coffee," Serena replied dryly as she returned to the swing. "And instant, at that."

"Ah, but it's the thought that counts." Alex's eyes, as they moved over her face, had the impact of a physical caress. "Have I told you this morning that you're absolutely lovely?"

She forced herself to remain calm as he put the cup down on a small table and squatted down in front of her. His bare, muscular legs were only inches from her own. "I believe we've covered that topic."

His hand lightly cupped the back of her neck. "Did I tell you that your perfume drives me crazy?"

Serena's mouth went suddenly dry. "I'm not wearing any perfume."

Alex nodded knowingly. "I was afraid that was the case. You realize, of course, that makes you even more dangerous."

You're the dangerous one, Serena could have said. Instead, she reminded herself that to Alex, this was nothing more than a well-rehearsed game designed to make life more interesting. She suspected that he played it often. And well.

"I'm only offering coffee this morning," she reminded him. "Nothing more."

He rocked forward on the balls of his feet. "Did anyone ever tell you that you take life far too seriously?" His smile was guileless. "Would you care to hear my theory?"

"Not really."

His grin widened. "Sorry, I seem to be in a mood to wax philosphical this morning, so you're going to hear it anyway." His fingers were caressing the soft skin below her ear. "Life, Serena, my sweet, is a banquet. A smorgasbord. In order to enjoy it to the fullest, one should sample all it has to offer."

Her eyes flashed with barely restrained irritation. "I'm not on the menu, Alex. You'd save a great deal of time and effort by getting that through your head right now."

Before he could respond, the sound of a car engine disturbed the still morning air. Both glanced around to view Donovan's ancient M.G. turning the corner.

"Such a waste," Alex said with a sigh, rising reluctantly to his feet. His dark eyes took another prolonged tour of her body, giving Serena the impression that he could see through the bulky folds of Donovan's robe. "Perhaps I can change your mind before you leave Claremont."

Serena drew the lapels of the robe even closer together as Donovan pulled into the driveway. "Don't bet on it."

He chuckled as he leaned over and tugged on her hair. "I'm not normally a gambling man, Serena. But I'd bet every cent the college is paying me that we'll make love before you depart our quaint little town."

"Don't," she whispered, appalled by the way his words created an enervating flood of desire.

Alex studied her, drinking in the soft rose flush darkening the triangle of skin at the open throat of her robe. Her gray eyes struggled against a yearning that echoed his own and as he experienced a sudden, unreasonable urge to take her here, now, in the cool crisp air, Alex had to remind himself that Donovan would be coming out of the garage at any moment. Despite the inadvisability of such behavior, he couldn't stop his mind from painting erotic pictures of her golden skin gleaming in the early-morning sunlight.

"You kept me awake last night," he murmured. His deep, lush voice wrapped Serena in its velvet embrace. "Do you have any idea how long it's been since I've lost sleep over a woman?"

When she didn't respond, Alex continued. "I can't remember; perhaps never." His eyes darkened with something that resembled restrained anger more than desire. "What do you suggest we do about that, Serena Lawrence?"

Serena swallowed. "Nothing."

"That's your suggestion," he countered. "I have different plans."

Her eyes flew hopefully to the detached garage. What on earth was Donovan doing in there? Deciding that discretion was the better part of valor, Serena opted for retreat. She rose from the chair, shaking off his hand.

"I'm really not interested in your plans," she proclaimed coolly, turning away from him.

Alex's fingers cupped her shoulders as he turned her around, forestalling her escape. "You intrigue me, Serena."

"Tough," she flared, angered by his blatant assumption that she was his for the taking. Like some ripe fruit to be casually plucked from the vine.

Alex felt a burst of satisfaction. He had finally gotten through those layers of reserve. He couldn't remember anything exciting him as much as that fire blazing in her eyes. He was admittedly an impatient man, but he could bide his time when something was worth waiting for. And Serena Lawrence definitely fit into that category.

He glanced down at his watch. "Much as I hate to leave just when the conversation's getting interesting, I do have a class."

Unable to resist touching her, he trailed his fingers up her forearm, slipping them under the folded-back sleeve of the robe. Her pulse, in the crook of her elbow, beat wildly. Alex wanted to press his lips against that soft, fragrant skin.

"Later," he said as he reluctantly relinquished possession of her arm.

"No."

His smile was dazzling, beguiling and oh-so-very-dangerous. Serena flinched as he brushed her bangs off her forehead with a casual gesture. "Don't frown so," he admonished gently, smoothing her furrowed brow with his fingertips. "You wouldn't want to make wrinkles in that gorgeous skin."

Alex picked up his coffee cup and turned away, tossing Donovan, who had finally come out of the garage, a welcoming grin. "Quite some sister you've got there."

Donovan's interested gaze moved from Alex to Serena and back again. "I've always thought so," he agreed.

"I'll see you around eight for dinner, Serena," Alex called back from his own porch. "Don't worry if your suitcase doesn't show up; we can always go someplace casual."

He was inside the small, pumpkin-colored house before Serena could assure him that she had absolutely no intention of going anywhere with him this evening. Casual or otherwise.

3

FRUSTRATED, SERENA TURNED on her brother. "It's about time you got home."

Donovan grinned as he sprawled on the swing. "If you ask me, I arrived just in time to screw things up." He eyed Serena appraisingly. "I've heard the guy's a fast worker, but it's always edifying to watch an expert in action."

She glared at him. "Why do men always stick together?"

"Simple. Survival."

Her only response was an unladylike snort.

"He really is a nice guy, Serena," Donovan offered. "Once you get to know him."

"I have no intention of getting to know him," she responded stiffly. "I have far more important things to think about than that Middle Eastern Casanova."

The smile faded from his eyes as they dropped down to her arm. "Are you sure you're all right?"

"My arm's fine." *Knock on wood*, she added mentally.

"I was referring to life in general. How's everything really going with you, runt?"

At the familiar nickname, Serena sank down beside him on the swing. She could feel the tears welling up behind her lids. Despite the fact that Donovan was not a blood relative, he had always been the one individual Serena had turned to in times of crisis. Not that he ever volunteered any solutions to her problems or forced his opinions on her. Instead, he would simply remain quietly supportive, allowing Serena to sort out her own answer. Donovan Kincaid had always been her refuge, her anchor in an uncertain sea, and it had broken her heart when their parents had divorced shortly before her twelfth birthday.

Serena had been eight years old when her mother, Margaret Winningham Brookshire Lawrence, had married Michael Kincaid, Donovan's father. At the time, the adults involved had decided that Serena would live with her father during the school year. After all, it would never do for her to be away from her tennis coach. William Lawrence, in turn, had agreed that Serena would spend twelve weeks every summer in California with her mother.

That first summer Donovan had been, in Serena's eyes, a handsome, wildly mature thirteen-year-old. She developed an immediate crush on her stepbrother, following him everywhere like a faithful puppy. In later years Serena would look back on her behavior and marvel that Donovan had never uttered a word of complaint. He had allowed her to tag along to the movies and the beach with his friends, who inevitably grew accustomed to having the leggy, freckle-faced kid along.

The summer Donovan turned sixteen and got his driver's license, Serena discovered she was suddenly not welcome on his dates. In the beginning she had sulked childishly, refusing to talk to him. But Donovan had remained undaunted, never failing to bring her home some small trinket. A wildflower from his waterskiing trip to Lake Arrowhead, long ropes of red licorice from the movies, a Mickey Mouse charm bracelet from Disneyland. Oh, yes, Serena thought now with a sigh, while she had survived all her mother's marriages and subsequent divorces, the hardest blow had come the year her mother had divorced Michael Kincaid and the summer visits had ceased.

"Serena?" Donovan's concerned voice broke into her introspection.

Serena shook her head to clear it. "Sorry. I was just think-ing." What had he asked? How she was, Serena remem-bered. "I think my arm is almost one hundred percent."

He took her hand in his, linking their fingers together. "I told you that I wasn't asking about your arm," he reminded her quietly. "I can read that in any sports magazine. I was asking about you."

She smiled gamely. "I'll know in three weeks. If I win, then I'll be fine."

Donovan returned her smile, but his eyes remained seri-ous. "There's more to life than tennis, Serena. I would have thought the past two years would have taught you that."

Serena bristled. "The past two years have only demon-strated that tennis *is* my life," she countered. "If I hadn't be-lieved I could play again, I wouldn't have had any incentive to keep going."

Donovan ignored the stiff warning in her tone, continuing to press his case. "What about a family? A husband? Per-haps a couple of kids? Don't you ever think about that?" He gave her a boyish smile that admitted he was intruding into her personal matters and had every intention of continuing. "Let's face it, kiddo, you're not getting any younger, you know."

"That's terrific, coming from the surrogate father to a bunch of monkeys. Apes," she corrected as sudden storm threatened to extinguish the light in his eyes. "Besides, you're five years older than I am, brother dear. And unless I over-looked them in all that clutter, you don't have a wife and kiddies stashed around this house anywhere."

"That doesn't mean I haven't been thinking about starting a family."

Serena crossed her arms over her chest. "I see. I suppose that luscious redhead is one of the candidates? Somehow, she didn't strike me as the maternal type."

Donovan had the grace to grin sheepishly. "In the first place, runt, we spent the night sitting up with a sick friend." At Serena's disbelieving expression, he added, "Honest. You remember Gloria, the *Gorilla gorilla beringei* I've been working with, don't you? She hasn't been sleeping very well lately and Dr. Taylor thought she might be able to help."

Serena arched a delicate brow. "*Dr.* Taylor? What's her specialty?"

"Biology."

"It figures," Serena said dryly.

Donovan chuckled good-naturedly. "Don't be catty. In case you haven't noticed, women are allowed to be attractive *and* astute these days. Paula just happens to be a vibrant, intelligent woman who is also interested in my work."

"Among other things. I *saw* how she was looking at you, Donovan. If you had been a Milky Way bar, you would have been a goner."

"At least I'm not hiding from life," he answered easily. "Besides, if I remember correctly, we were talking about *your* future."

"We were," Serena agreed. "And while I'll admit it's a little uncertain at the moment, the one thing I know with an iron-clad certainty is that it does not—and never will—include marriage."

Donovan's smile faded to a thoughtful frown and his tanned forehead furrowed. "You sound as if you've definitely made up your mind about that."

"I have." Softening her tone, Serena sought to make him understand. "Donovan, how many marriages has your father had?"

He considered her question for a moment. "Three."

"Three," she repeated, as if that proved her point. "My mother has been married five times and before I left the clinic I received a letter informing me that she's going to make it an even half dozen. Some duke with an orange orchard in Seville. I wouldn't want to live that way." Tight lines bracketed her lips. "I refuse to live that way."

Donovan stroked her arm. "Hey, admittedly, neither Pop nor your mom have done very well in the matrimonial sweepstakes. But they don't represent the norm," he reminded her. "What about all those couples who don't get divorced?"

"The ones who belong in *Ripley's Believe it or Not*?" Serena's voiced dripped sarcasm.

Donovan sighed. "I guess I never realized you'd grown up to be so bitter, runt."

"Not bitter. Just grown up."

Serena was surprised to see that Donovan was honestly distressed by the conversation. Not wanting to spoil their reunion, she leaned over and kissed his cheek.

"Besides, right now I've got to concentrate on getting my career back on track. In three weeks I'm going to show the world that the rumors of Serena Lawrence's demise are greatly exaggerated. In order to do that, I'm going to have to get in a lot of practice.

"Then, after I prove myself in the charity match, it's on to Italy. Then the French Open. Then Wimbledon. I can't even contemplate a relationship with any man until I prove to everyone, including myself, that I can still play in Centre Court."

Donovan's bright green eyes lit with hope. "But after you make your comeback, promise me that you won't entirely discount the idea of a family, okay?"

Serena loved this man more than anyone in the entire world. How could she deny him anything? "I'll give it some thought." It wasn't precisely the truth, but she didn't want to argue with her brother. She knew she had made the right decision when he grinned happily.

"That's my girl." He ruffled her hair affectionately. "Why don't you come talk to me while I dig up something for breakfast? Then we can go check on Gloria." He glanced up at the robin's-egg-blue sky. "It's a gorgeous day, how do you feel about walking over there?"

It had been several years since Serena had visited the primate center at the far eastern edge of the campus. At the time, workmen had been expanding the compound that housed Donovan's family of apes.

"I'd love to, it's been too long since I've seen your motley crew of monkeys." As a brief scowl flittered across her brother's features, Serena laughed. "Just kidding," she said sweetly.

SERENA STARED at the huge female gorilla whose dark eyes were glued to a wide-screen television. "*Baretta*? In Japanese?"

"We've got a satellite dish that picks up signals from all over the world. Gloria's been allowed to change her own channels for the past month and she keeps flipping through them until she finds a police show." Donovan's gaze turned thoughtful. "I haven't determined the sociological implications of that yet."

When a commercial for shampoo came on the screen, Gloria hooted her irritation. Pictures flashed by as she angrily punched the buttons of the channel selector. When she located a syndicated German version of *Mod Squad*, Gloria grunted happily, her attention once again riveted on the oversize screen.

"How old is Gloria?"

"Six," Donovan answered immediately. He looked over at her curiously. "Why?"

"Because the sociological implication is obvious, even to a novice," Serena said. "If her viewing habits stay the same in a few years you're going to have a teenage delinquent on your hands, brother dear."

"Paula believes she may be suffering a chemical imbalance," Donovan said thoughtfully.

"Pooh." Serena slipped her hand through his arm, leading him away from the compound. "The only thing Gloria is suffering from is a serious attack of bad taste. My prescription is to take that remote control away from her and start her on a daily dose of *Masterpiece Theater*."

Donovan laughed appreciatively. "Do you know, that's the precise thing Alex suggested?"

Serena froze at the sudden intrusion of Donovan's disturbing neighbor into their light banter. "Really," she said coolly, her tone not inviting Donovan to elaborate.

"Really." He grinned down at her. "Looks as if you two have something in common."

"That'll be the day," she muttered.

Leaving Donovan with his apes, Serena returned to the house just in time to greet the airline employee returning her errant luggage. She changed from yesterday's clothing into a pair of yellow shorts and a grass-green T-shirt then settled onto the swing with a best-selling paperback novel. Several minutes later, she hadn't gotten past the first page; her gaze kept shifting to the house next door. Thoroughly disgusted with her lack of self-control, Serena decided to walk the frustrating man out of her thoughts.

As she strolled idly down the ivy-edged sidewalk, Serena swung her arm tentatively to test her elbow. She hated the way her arm had become such a focal point in her life. She was never entirely free of pain, nor had she been for the past two years. The best she could say was that at least nowadays she didn't cry herself to sleep each night.

Playing with the pain was nothing new for Serena. She remembered times that her shoulder or her knee or some other joint had been aching, yet she had managed to play beyond the pain, winning the tournament despite her injury. Any athlete not willing to play with pain was an athlete who didn't play. This time, however, it was different. This time her entire life revolved around her arm. Her future depended on its strength.

Serena knew that her career was now at its most crucial point. If she returned to the tour, she would be putting herself on the line day after day in a game that required self-discipline and allowed no excuses. She was no longer the little girl with nerves of steel who had taken the world by storm.

Nor was she the composed young woman who had been dubbed the Ice Princess due to her remarkable control on the court. Now she was simply a twenty-eight-year-old woman with an arm that hurt. And as the time came to put that arm to the test, Serena found herself growing more and more apprehensive.

As she passed the north gate of the campus, Serena paused to read the inscription carved into the stone. Let Only the Eager, Thoughtful and Reverent Enter Here. Well, she was certainly eager. And since the accident, she had definitely grown thoughtful. In fact, her deep introspection had recently been proving more of a liability than an asset. Serena knew she had been allowing herself to dwell on the might-have-beens, which was a grievous error. Reverent? Well, two out of three wasn't bad.

The college, its curriculum patterned after that of Oxford, had been established in the late nineteenth century by Althea D. Smiley to prove that coeducation and excellence in education were indeed compatible. While the institution's diplomas still bore the lengthy name given it by its early feminist founder, The Althea D. Smiley Coeducational College was more often referred to simply as Smiley College.

The first time Serena had visited Donovan at Smiley, she had felt as if someone had sneaked a bit of New England into California while all the natives were at the beach. The park-like campus provided a quiet and spacious setting for the ivy-covered buildings. The serene grounds served to soothe Serena's turmoil. When she sat down on the edge of one of the fountains and watched the California sun making rainbows in the sparkling water, her tension slowly melted away.

Returning down Harvard Avenue toward Donovan's house, her spirits lifted, Serena failed to notice the couple who stopped to stare at her before hurrying to the pay telephone on the corner.

ALEX WAS NOT AT ALL PLEASED with the way his classes had gone. Starting out poorly with his nine o'clock lecture, they had deteriorated significantly as the day progressed. Normally, a lecture on Middle East oil reserves would be a cakewalk; he could do it in his sleep. But his mind had continually wandered, conjuring up images of Serena Lawrence.

He imagined unwrapping her from those voluminous folds of Donovan's burgundy robe, slowly, tenderly. He envisioned making love to her in a myriad of ways and places: in the sparkling California sunshine, under a gleaming canopy of stars, on the beach, in the Victorian gazebo in his backyard, in front of a fire in a cabin on the top of the snow-capped mountains located only minutes from the campus.

Alex was stunned by how Serena had managed to infiltrate every corner of his mind, disturbing first his sleep and now his work. He wasn't certain he liked the idea of any woman having such power over him. When he couldn't remember the succession of Iran's Peacock Throne on two separate occasions, Alex realized he was stumbling badly and dismissed his afternoon class early, giving up for the day. Although the students were obviously puzzled, no one objected to getting a head start on the weekend.

Alex swiftly calculated how long it had been since he had spent an evening alone with a beautiful woman. Too long, he decided. Despite reassurances from friends that southern California was a haven for free-spirited individuals who would prove every bit as amiable as those in Washington,

D.C., his time had at first been occupied by locating and moving into his house.

Then there had been lecture schedules to devise, classes to teach, essays to mark, not to mention the rounds of seemingly unending social functions that had proven to be part and parcel of the academic life. The diplomatic corps might have elevated the working cocktail party to a fine art, but Alex had belatedly discovered that governments were pikers when compared to colleges and the political atmosphere generated in collegiate social gatherings.

That was all that was wrong, Alex assured himself. He was simply reacting so uncharacteristically to Serena because he was in need of a woman. It had nothing to do with Serena personally. As the idea took root, Alex felt infinitely better.

While many men did not like the little intrigues constituting relationships between the sexes, he had always found such games amusing. Part of his enjoyment admittedly stemmed from the fact that he was very, very good at them. The only rule was there were no rules. Spontaneity was the key, mutual pleasure the goal. Actually, Alex did possess one commandment that kept the contest from getting out of hand. Neither participant in the relationship would ever become serious or demand more than the other was willing to give.

Part of Alex's success with women lay in the fact that he truly liked them. Obviously enjoying their company, he always possessed a surfeit of willing, intelligent women. Women who were every bit as stimulating to talk with over the breakfast table as they had been intriguing over a candlelit dinner the night before. A bit of a prodigy, he had given up on empty-headed beauties by the time he was nineteen.

Despite his admittedly vast experience with the opposite sex, Alex could not remember any woman affecting him with quite the same jolt as Serena Lawrence. As he walked home along College Avenue, he vowed to solve the problem with Serena before classes resumed on Monday morning. So lost was he in thought, he failed to notice the van bearing a network logo until it pulled up beside him.

"Excuse me." A man Alex vaguely recognized as a sportscaster for a Los Angeles television station smiled at him. "I'm afraid we're lost."

"Happens all the time," Alex agreed politely. Actually, because the town was laid out on a grid, it was very difficult to lose your way. But after all these years, diplomacy was second nature.

"Perhaps you can help us," the man suggested hopefully.

"I'll try."

When the sportscaster read Donovan Kincaid's address off his notepad, Alex's mind spun into high gear. He began rattling off a complicated series of instructions, which, if followed to the letter, would take the van in the opposite direction, away from Donovan's house. As soon as the news team resumed their quest, Alex ran across the street to the Montgomery Art Building, where he used the telephone at the front desk to call Serena.

"Hello?"

Serena rifled through the stacks of papers on the desk, searching for a pen to take a message for her brother. She hadn't seen Donovan since leaving him in the lab, where he was lost in plotting data. Knowing his proclivity to lose track of time, she doubted if she would see him again before tomorrow morning.

"Serena, I'm glad I caught you at home," Alex said abruptly, dispensing with pleasantries.

She experienced an unwelcome flare of pleasure at the familiar deep voice. "Alex?"

"You didn't agree to a television interview today, did you?"

The very idea created a knot in the pit of her stomach. "Of course not. Why do you ask?"

"Because there's a news crew headed your way."

"Oh, no." Serena didn't want to talk to them. She didn't want to answer the inevitable questions about her arm. Her attempted comeback. Brett. But she knew that if she didn't, they'd camp out in Donovan's front yard, effectively holding her hostage until she surrendered.

"Don't worry, it's going to take them a while to find you," Alex said. "Go over to my place. There's a spare key under the mat."

"That's not very imaginative; it's probably the first place a burglar would look."

"While you're waiting for me to get home you can occupy your time thinking up a new hiding place," he suggested dryly.

Serena possessed the good grace to flinch at his gritty tone. After all, he had gone to all the trouble of warning her.

"I'm sorry. It's none of my business where you hide your key."

Her soft tone eased his irritation. "I'll be there in five minutes. Then we'll work out an escape plan." He started to hang up.

"Alex?"

"Yes?"

Her voice revealed her confusion. "Why are you doing this?" Serena reluctantly admitted that nothing in her behavior had encouraged him to treat her so thoughtfully.

"Simple. I've been there."

Not wanting to waste any more time, Alex hung up the receiver and headed out of the building on a run.

4

SERENA WAS WAITING for Alex when he arrived. "Ready to go?" he asked.

"Go where?"

"Anywhere. Since I promised to take you to dinner tonight, I thought we might drive into Los Angeles and get something to eat. By the time we get back to Claremont, your watchdogs will be gone."

Serena decided that it was definitely not the time to inform Alex that she had never intended to have dinner with him in the first place. "How do you know that?"

Alex glanced out the front window, his dark eyes scanning the street for the van. "Because it'll be too late for the newscast," he stated with exaggerated patience. "If we don't get going, we're not going to make it out of here before they unscramble those false directions I gave them."

"You gave them the wrong directions?" Serena stared up at him. "Really?"

The motion of his jaw suggested Alex was grinding his teeth. "We're wasting time here, Serena."

"Nice car," she offered a moment later as he opened the garage door to reveal a sleek black Jaguar convertible. "But don't you think we're going to be a little conspicuous?"

He arched a black brow. "In southern California?"

Serena laughed at that. "You've got a point."

They passed the news van as they approached the access to the San Bernardino Freeway. Despite the fact that Alex had put the top up on the convertible, Serena slid down in the passenger seat and crossed her fingers, hoping that the men inside the van wouldn't spot her. But they were too busy scrutinizing addresses, the blistering scowls on their faces betraying the fact that Alex's convoluted directions had succeeded in getting them even more lost than before.

"I love it!" Serena clapped her hands as they escaped onto the freeway with a roar of the powerful engine. "I feel just like Bonnie and Clyde!"

Alex glanced over at her as he changed lanes, merging into the steady stream of traffic. Her eyes were bright with dancing lights, her face wreathed in a brilliant smile.

"You should do that more often."

Serena's smile faded. "Do what?"

"Smile. You're beautiful when you smile, Serena Lawrence."

Serena didn't know why that simple statement, which she was certain Alex uttered to women on a daily, if not hourly basis, should cause her to feel so uncomfortable, but it did. Instinctively her voice turned a little cooler and her gray eyes were tinged with frost.

"As opposed to the rest of the time?"

"I wouldn't have thought that with all you have going for yourself, you'd be so insecure that you couldn't accept a compliment gracefully." He spoke without rancor as he kept his gaze directed out the front windshield.

"Do you know that no one, in all the years I've been playing tennis, has ever suggested that I have a less than Olympian ego?"

"That's what's usually said about me."

Serena refused to consider that she had just stumbled across one more thing she and Alex Bedare had in common. "I can certainly believe that." Because her words sounded harsh, even to her own ears, Serena softened her tone. "I do want to thank you for rescuing me, though. It was a very nice thing to do."

His smile flashed under his black mustache. "I've always been a sucker for beautiful ladies in distress."

As they drove along in silence, Alex debated where to take Serena for dinner. This afternoon he had settled on Les Anges, the simple and pretty pastel place in Santa Monica Canyon. The food was late nouvelle cuisine—very good, very inventive and very expensive. It was just the place to take a lady you wanted to impress. Then afterward, he had planned to take Serena for a moonlight stroll along the beach.

His plan had been simple. Lower her defenses with food, weaken her resistance with moonlight and satisfy what he knew to be their shared desire. Then he could get on with his life, content to regard Serena as merely another appealing woman friend.

"I'm not exactly dressed for Les Anges," Serena demurred when Alex suggested the restaurant to her.

His dark eyes flicked over her. "I suppose not, now that you mention it. Although on you, that T-shirt looks good. Is that your credo?" he asked as he read the message printed across the front. He Who Dies with the Most Toys Wins.

"No. It was a gift from a friend."

Serena turned her head, directing her gaze out the passenger window as she displayed a sudden interest in a red Ferrari in the outside lane. It wasn't the way she viewed life at all. It had, however, been the way Brett had lived his. He had bought the T-shirt in a shop on Rodeo Drive, giving it to Serena as a gag birthday gift. Two days later, all she had left of her friend was the shirt and bittersweet memories. Memories that Serena was not prepared to discuss with Alex.

Alex couldn't miss the way her fingers were twisting together in her lap. Now what had he said? Deciding not to press her, he refrained from commenting.

"Where are we going?" Serena asked, finally breaking the heavy silence.

"How do you feel about a picnic on the beach?"

Serena privately thought it was a ridiculous idea. While the spring days were warm, the nights were cool. In the interest of avoiding an argument, she kept her opinion to herself.

"Sounds nice," she murmured noncommittally.

"Huntington has fire pits, if you're worried about the cold," he assured her. "And I keep a blanket in the trunk."

Handy, Serena thought. "I'm not worried. But what about your clothes?" While she wasn't properly dressed for a romantic restaurant, neither was a three-piece suit usual beach attire.

Alex shrugged. "I'm sure the dry cleaner can manage to repair whatever damage might occur."

The silence settled over them again, but this time it did not seem so stultifying. In fact, Serena considered with some surprise, it was almost companionable. She waited in the car as Alex stopped at a delicatessen a few blocks from the beach where he purchased sandwiches, Greek salad and wood for the fire pit. Before long, they were seated on the blanket, the blazing fire sending sparks into the indigo sky.

To Serena's surprise, their dinner conversation flowed easily. They discussed Alex's work at the college; Donovan's primate studies, which were achieving worldwide interest; southern California, an area they both viewed as a natural extension of Disneyland; and London, a city they discovered that they had in common. While Serena had spent most of her childhood in the nearby countryside of Essex, Alex had studied at Oxford, visiting London often. Including, he informed her, the two times he had watched her win the Wimbledon singles final.

"This was a terrific idea," Serena admitted much later as she sipped clove-spiced orange tea from a Styrofoam cup. "I can't remember when I've felt so relaxed."

Alex leaned back on his elbows, studying her judiciously. The taut lines that had bracketed her lips on more than one occasion had vanished. Her gray eyes, as they looked out

over the moon-gilded expanse of the Pacific Ocean, possessed a dreamlike quality. She appeared much more at ease.
And worlds more approachable.

"I'm glad to hear that. I think you needed to unwind a bit."

As the soft sea breeze tousled her sleek cap of blond hair
to casual disorder, he leaned forward, brushing a few shimmering strands back from her face. The gesture, which had
begun innocently enough, seemed strangely intimate. He
could almost feel her skin warming under his fingertips. A
heat that had nothing to do with the nearby fire. A heat that
was echoed deep within his own body.

As their eyes locked, Serena was stunned, not for the first
time, by the way Alex's touch had created such a flare within
her. All he had done was brush her windblown hair out of her
eyes. A harmless enough gesture. So why had he left her
feeling so shaken? Serena had never been one to fool herself
and she wasn't about to begin now. It was desire, she admitted secretly. Pure, unadulterated lust.

Once she had diagnosed the sensation, Serena found it no
longer disturbed her. In truth, it was a relief to discover that
she could feel something—anything—besides fear and mis-
giving. It demonstrated that her spirit, as well as her body,
was mending. Serena had submerged her emotions well during the past two years, hiding them even from herself while
concentrating on rehabilitating her arm. This sexual jolt,
which she had no intention of doing anything about, was
oddly reassuring.

Alex recalled his fantasy of lying with Serena on the plaid
blanket, her tanned skin gleaming amber and gold in the glow
of the firelight. Not wanting to do anything to frighten her
away, he retreated from the inviting scenario for the time.

"As pleasant as this evening has been," he said, "we can't
keep skipping town every time a news crew drives down your
street. If you're serious about returning to the tour, Serena,
you're going to have to talk to the press sooner or later."

"Do we have to talk about that tonight?" she asked with a deep sigh. "We've been having such a nice time. At least I have," she added as an afterthought.

They appeared to be the only two people on the beach. The moonlight streamed like silent, silvery dust, making the sand sparkle like a million diamonds. The only sounds were the distant crash of the surf and the crackling of the flames. It was definitely a night made for romance. Fortunately—or unfortunately, Serena's rebellious mind couldn't decide which— Alex appeared to have abandoned his seduction attempts. She wondered if she had already managed to bore him.

Alex did not miss the question in her voice. "So have I. After our conversation this morning, I'm a little surprised. I figured you'd spend the entire evening imitating a porcupine."

She threw him a mock scowl. "Do you know, I'm having an extremely difficult time envisioning you as a diplomat. That was not a very tactful statement."

He frowned, knowing her words to be the truth. He had spent years learning to use language precisely. Yet since meeting Serena, all his skills seemed to have flown out the window.

"Which would you prefer?" he asked. "Diplomacy? Or the truth?" He spoke quietly, his eyes moving to her mouth.

Serena's nerves were suddenly stretched tight. He was testing her, issuing a challenge that she could easily turn away from, ending this conversation right now. Or she could accept. And take the consequences. She waited to speak until she was certain she had control of her voice.

"Are the two incompatible?"

Alex gave her points for composure. She was good, he mused. Very, very good. He decided it came from all those years of repressing her emotions on the tennis court. Alex experienced a sense of excitement as he returned her verbal volley.

"Usually, where women are concerned."

When he suddenly leaned forward, Serena drew in a quick breath, expecting to be touched. But instead he merely tossed another piece of wood onto the fire. A flurry of orange sparks flew upward, disappearing into the black sky.

"Can't have you getting cold," he explained with an entirely false smile. He lay back down, his arms behind his head as he stared up at the vast expanse of sky. "Look at those stars," he murmured, as if to himself. "You could almost reach up and touch them."

Serena murmured an agreement, but she wasn't looking at the stars. Her eyes were drinking in the sight of Alex, stretched out on the blue and black blanket. He had discarded his jacket and vest immediately upon arriving at the beach and the pristine white shirt superbly molded the hard lines of his body. Removing his gold cuff links, he had rolled his shirt-sleeves up to just below the elbows, exposing firm forearms graced with ebony hair similar to those curly dark strands filling in the V of his open collar.

Knowing it was a dangerous move, Serena allowed her surreptitious gaze to travel down Alex's long legs. The continental style of his trousers only served to emphasize the strong thighs, well corded with taut muscles she had observed this morning, when he had been clad in those brief jogging shorts.

Alex turned his head toward Serena just as her gaze was returning to his face. She was trembling despite the warmth of the fire. And her wide gray eyes were far from calm. Even as he realized he had achieved some measure of control over Serena, Alex was forced to admit such success was not entirely one-sided. His own heart was pounding furiously.

"Come here." His voice was a lush velvet ribbon of sound, while his dark eyes beckoned her nearer, inviting her to drown in the deep ebony pools.

Serena's mouth went dry; words deserted her. She shook her head as she drew her knees to her chest and wrapped her arms around them.

Alex did not argue. Instead he sat up, one hand reaching out to smooth her tense shoulder. When she shuddered under his touch, he murmured some soothing words in a language that she took to be Arabic. While Serena couldn't translate those words, their seductive meaning was unmistakable. When that treacherous hand trailed down her arm, Serena instructed herself to pull away. Now. But she remained rooted to the spot, intrigued in spite of herself as to what Alex intended to do next.

He pried her fingers loose—one hand at a time—then, with a gesture that caused liquid heat to flow through her veins, he lifted each tingling fingertip to his lips. He took his time, his eyes not leaving hers as he kissed them slowly, one at a time, before pressing a provocative kiss against the tender skin of her palm. Serena's blood leaped in response.

Releasing her hand, Alex cupped his long, dark fingers under her chin. Without utilizing a modicum of force, he drew her to him with only that light, enticing touch. Serena heard a soft, resigned sigh and failed to realize that it had escaped her own lips.

She gasped at the initial contact. Serena had kissed men before. Despite her devout dedication to her sport, she was not totally without experience. Still, she wasn't prepared for the explosion that rocketed through her as her mouth met his. When she tried to pull away, Alex shook his head.

"No," he said. "Not yet."

His eyes were liquid ebony, brightened by the reflected glow of the firelight. As they settled on her trembling lips, Serena's resistance melted away, like the foundation of a sand castle at high tide. Reading her acceptance, Alex returned his mouth to hers.

As he kissed her wonderfully, lingeringly, Serena found herself wrapped in a warm cocoon of sensual pleasure. His mustache brushed against her tender skin, creating sparks before moving on to torment her cheek, her temple, her closed eyelids. She cried out as his tongue traced a ring of fire around the perimeter of her softly parted lips. He still hadn't touched her; their only contact was their mouths, mobile, clinging, capable of the most extraordinary pleasures.

Serena's mouth grew hot, avid, as she returned Alex's kisses with unrestrained passion. She ran her fingers through his hair, breathing in the piquant scent of smoke that lingered in the ebony strands.

Much, much later—it could have been minutes, hours or an eternity—Alex released her lips. His dark gaze drank in her flushed, softened features. "I knew it."

"Knew what?"

"I knew there was fire under all that ice."

Serena knew it would be useless to deny his words. Not after what they had just shared. "That fire just happens to be what makes me a winner."

He arched a brow as he trailed his fingers idly over her cheekbone. "And the ice? What does it do?"

"The ice, as you insist on calling it, keeps me in control. It keeps me from losing."

"And you never lose."

Her smooth tone handed him a warning. "Never."

Alex framed her sternly set face with his palms. "Neither do I." His expression was thoughtful. "I wonder where, exactly, that leaves us?"

'Nowhere," she insisted. "I've already told you, Alex, I have no intention of having an affair with you."

"You know what they say about the best-laid plans."

Serena shook her head. The man simply refused to listen. "Are you always this impossible?"

"Always. That's what made *me* a winner at the negotiation tables. I never give up." His eyes sparkled with unrepressed humor. "Serena?"

"What is it now?" she snapped, irritated by the way he seemed to consider her honest objections nothing more than intriguing obstacles to be overcome.

Alex ran a finger down her cheek. "I really do love your smile."

Serena's lips curved upward in an instinctive response. "Damn you," she protested. "You don't fight fair."

He grinned before pressing a kiss against her mouth. The brief flare ended all too soon. "I never said I did, love. I never said I did."

WHAT WAS THE WOMAN doing to his mind? Four days had passed since Alex had first encountered Serena Lawrence hiding in the shrubbery at that fund-raising party. Four long days and four equally long, sleepless nights. There was so much he should be doing: planning lectures, grading essays, preparing for the government conference on Middle Eastern terrorism he had agreed to chair in Washington at the end of the month. So many things demanded his undivided attention. So why couldn't he stop thinking of her?

What was it about Serena that tantalized him as no other woman had ever done? At this very moment, he was seated at his rolltop desk, staring out the window toward Donovan's house instead of working, as he should be. The yellow legal pad was covered with lopsided squares, giving mute proof of his inattention.

She was lovely, yes. But Alex knew other women just as beautiful. She was intelligent, but no more so than any other woman of his acquaintance. She was maddeningly stubborn and ambitious to the point of being obsessive about her career. But despite all this, Alex found himself even more intrigued.

He sighed as his pen switched to circles. What would it be like to have Serena's passion for tennis directed his way? The memory of the kiss they had shared had ballooned in his mind, teasing him with sensual suggestions that were proving more frustrating with each passing day.

Cursing her heatedly and wanting her outrageously, Alex threw down his pen and left the house, determined to walk off these atypical feelings of unrest.

SERENA SPENT MUCH of her free time walking around the campus, contemplating her return to tennis. The upcoming charity tournament would provide a long-awaited test. If her arm maintained its strength and control, as she hoped it would, her career would be back on track. If not . . . Serena refused to consider the possibility.

Something even more disturbing than her concern over her return to the tour was the way Alex seemed to have infiltrated himself into her thoughts. She could not allow herself to fall under his seductive spell. A lifetime of experience, both on and off the court, had taught Serena that everything was transient, temporary. Here today, gone tomorrow. Matches, tournaments, relationships. Nothing was forever. Especially relationships.

In that respect, Serena had always found tennis perfectly suited to her temperament. Unlike other sports, it was a game in which a player had no teammates. Tennis was an individual effort; you won or lost by yourself. Laughed or cried by yourself. The press had frequently described Serena as a loner. She had decided long ago that the term fit.

On the fifth day of her stay in Claremont, Serena woke to find the town enveloped in fog. Muttering under her breath, she pulled a sweat suit on over her shorts and T-shirt. With any luck it would burn off in an hour or so, but one never knew. While it wouldn't interfere with her practicing her ground strokes, the dampness in the air was less than ideal for her arm.

She put a bucket of balls onto the passenger seat of Donovan's M.G. and drove the few short blocks to the college tennis courts, which her brother had arranged for her to use every morning from seven until noon. Unfortunately, her longtime coach, Marty Jennings, had met with a skiing accident last week. At this moment he was in a Sun Valley hospital, unable to practice with her.

Marty had admittedly done his best to make it up to Serena. With a few telephone calls he had managed to round up a few of the better amateurs in Claremont for her to practice with, but the resulting sessions had been less than challenging. Today she was working out on her own. While it was a less than ideal situation, no other solution had presented itself.

Despite the coolness of the early-morning air, after ten minutes of exertion, Serena shrugged off her jacket. She hit the balls against a back wall again and again, hardly pausing for breath. William Lawrence had taught Serena at an early age that concentration was born on the practice courts. She had learned to ignore everything but the ball and her racket.

The sudden squeal of brakes shattered the still morning air, followed by the blare of a car horn and heated cursing as the driver of a late-model Trans Am barely missed hitting a bicyclist who had swerved into his lane. A squirrel chattered stridently from the top branches of an oak tree nearby and there was a roar of approval from the direction of the swimming pool as the college water-polo team scored another point in their early-morning practice session. Serena remained blissfully unaware of it all.

"You're raising your shoulder on that backhand."

The deep, all too familiar voice shattered her concentration. Serena allowed the ball to go skidding past her as she spun around to face Alex. *Stop that*, she instructed her facial muscles, which seemed to have developed a mind of their own as they insisted on smiling at him.

"I didn't realize your vast talents included tennis coaching."

"I've played a bit, although I wouldn't begin to claim to be in your class," he hastened to add. "However, I've always admired your backhand. That's the only reason I could tell that it's not quite the same today."

Serena realized the man had just given her a compliment devoid of sexual invitation. He had also given her some valuable advice. She probably was lifting her shoulder to compensate for her weak elbow. She'd have to watch that carefully.

"Thanks," she said.

As Serena moved nearer the fence, she noticed Alex was dressed more informally today. While the gray flannel slacks were expensively tailored and the crease could have cut diamonds, they were more casual than either the three-piece suit or the tuxedo he had been wearing when they met. The Harris tweed jacket boasted the obligatory suede elbow patches.

"You look more like a professor today."

"All I need is the pipe, right?"

Serena wrinkled her nose in a gesture that seemed ill-suited to the Ice Princess. "You can skip that. One of the doctors at the clinic smoked a Connemara pipe he'd picked up while attending a medical convention in Ireland. Whenever I smell pipe tobacco, I think of those rehabilitative exercises."

"I can see where that would be distressing," Alex agreed. "I'm glad I never developed the habit."

Serena shrugged. "You certainly wouldn't have to quit on my account." When he didn't answer immediately, she began absently bouncing the ball with her racket. Plunk. Plunk. The sound filled the growing silence. "After all, I'm only going to be around here another couple of weeks." Plunk.

Plunk. Plunk. "And if the past two days were any indication, we certainly won't be seeing much of each other."

Alex thought he detected an accusation in her quiet tone. "I thought I'd give you some time to think."

Serena began hitting the ball with increased vigor. "Think? About what?"

"Us."

She turned away, swinging her racket with a swift, strong stroke that drove the ball into the wall. "There isn't any *us*."

He slipped his hands into his pockets. "Of course there is," he argued amiably. "It doesn't do any good to deny it, Serena. Not after that kiss we shared Friday night."

Serena's eyes shot to his face. The ball flew by unnoticed. "That was a mistake."

"A mistake?" Alex's teeth flashed under his mustache. "I'd never be mistaken about such an important matter. I remember the incident very well, Serena. I kissed you. And you kissed me back."

Serena refused to continue the conversation another moment. She took another yellow ball from the bucket and smashed it into the wall. "Go away." As she returned it with a vicious backhand, Serena was careful to keep her shoulder down.

"Is that any way to talk to a man who's offering to let you destroy his male ego in order to further your own career?"

Damn the man, he was ruining her concentration! This time she hit the ball with the edge of the racket, sending it careening high into the air, over the fence, where it rolled under the wheels of a passing car.

"You owe me one tennis ball," she snapped, spinning back toward him. "What did you mean by that remark? I can't imagine even denting your masculine ego with anything less than a Sherman tank." She dropped a replacement ball and smacked it at the wall.

"Ouch. It seems I've failed to impress the lady with my silken charm."

Serena gave up on practicing, wishing she could break her tautly strung racket over the man's smug head. "I only have this court for five hours each day," she said briskly. "So in order not to waste any more time, why don't you simply tell me what you're talking about in one short, declarative sentence?"

Alex belatedly realized he had been taking up her valuable practice time. He hadn't considered the fact that Serena Lawrence couldn't practice just anywhere, anytime she liked, without drawing an unwelcome crowd.

"I'm sorry," he responded contritely. "While it's not exactly a declarative sentence, how's this: would the lovely and talented tennis professional settle for a less able but totally willing international-relations professor for a practice partner this morning?"

Serena stared at him. "You want to practice with me?"

"Unless you think I won't be able to give you enough of a game to make it worth your while." His coaxing smile was dazzling and appeared entirely sincere. "Donovan told me about your problem this morning, and while I'm admittedly far less proficient than your usual coach, I think I might be an improvement over that wall."

His warm smile did something funny to her; for a moment Serena felt as if she had drunk in a deep breath of pure oxygen. She almost dropped her racket.

"That would be a big help. If you have the time. Not having Marty here has made things a lot harder."

Serena didn't like remembering exactly how irritated Marty Jennings had been about her insistence on playing the upcoming charity match in the first place. Not believing her to be ready, he had counseled additional time. But after more than two years, Serena could not remain inactive any longer.

As it was, for the first time in her life, she was going into the major international tournaments unseeded.

Alex watched the shadow move across her eyes and was inexplicably moved. For a man famed for his witty repartee and his ability to know precisely the correct thing to say to a woman in any given circumstances, he found himself mo mentarily mute.

"I'll see you in a little over an hour," he promised finally "Right after my class."

"That'd be great. And Alex . . ."

"Yes?"

"Thanks. This will be the second time you've saved my life."

Serena's open smile, devoid of the icy remoteness he was accustomed to viewing on her face, struck Alex to the very core. Suddenly feeling like a tongue-tied adolescent, he feigned a casual shrug.

"I told you I've got a thing about damsels in distress. Be sides, trying to keep up with you is bound to improve my game."

He treated her to another of those devastating grins before taking off in the direction of Tanniger Hall. Serena watched until he turned the corner and disappeared from view. With a resigned sigh, she took yet another ball from the plastic bucket and hit it toward the concrete wall.

5

AN HOUR LATER, Serena had hit somewhere between four and five hundred balls. The California sun had burned away the fog and the day had blossomed sunny and warm. Although she had discarded the sweatpants long ago, Serena still felt unreasonably disheveled when Alex showed up, immaculate in white tennis shorts and a matching short-sleeved sweater.

Expecting merely a weekend tennis buff, Serena was surprised when, for the next two hours, Alex effectively ran her all over the court, changing speeds, bringing her to the net, forcing her back against the baseline. When the first class arrived at the court just as the bells in Smith Tower rang twelve times, Serena was ready to drop. The fact that she had taken two of the three sets was scant comfort to her rubbery legs.

"You should have warned me." She wiped her arms dry with a towel as they walked toward Donovan's M.G.

"Warned you?" Alex put the bucket of balls on the floor of the car.

"What's your California ranking?" Serena asked suspiciously.

"I'm not ranked. Are you giving me a ride back to my house?"

"I suppose so. I don't believe you."

Alex's smile was totally innocent as he fit his tall frame gingerly into the compact front seat. When there wasn't room on the floor for both his feet and the bucket of balls, he was forced to hold the bucket on his lap.

"I never asked what you did about that sportscaster," he said, adroitly changing the subject. "I haven't seen him skulking in the bushes around Donovan's house."

"I called him first thing Saturday morning and agreed to give him an exclusive interview before the charity match if he'd let me practice alone in peace. It seems to have worked. You're not going to get me off the track that easily, Alex. I want to know your California ranking."

"I'm telling you the truth, Serena," he protested. "I'm unranked here." When she opened her mouth to argue, he elaborated. "Of course I've only been in California a few months. I haven't played any tournaments. Yet."

"How about Washington?"

"Second," he admitted with a sheepish grin.

Serena nodded with satisfaction. "I thought so. And nationally?"

"Does it matter?"

"It does to me. I'd like to know exactly who it was who hustled me so smoothly out on that court this morning." She climbed into the driver's seat, jumping slightly as her bare thighs met the sun-warmed leather.

"I didn't hustle you," Alex protested. "We weren't playing for money. Besides, you won two out of three sets."

"Your ranking?" she insisted as she turned the key in the ignition.

"Twenty-second, in my age group."

"Only twenty-second?" she inquired dryly.

Alex ignored the sarcasm dripping from her voice. "I dropped a few points this past year. With all the disruptions in my life, I haven't had time to play."

As his words brought back his personal tragedy, Serena felt like the Wicked Witch of the West. "Well, at least you gave me more competition than I bargained for. My coach couldn't have run me any harder than you did back there," she accused.

"I thought that was the idea," Alex answered calmly.

Serena looked at him for a long, silent moment. The M.G. was idling quietly. "You're right," she agreed. "I was over-reacting, behaving like a poor loser."

Alex's dark eyes swept slowly over her face. "Impossible. You might give up a set or even a match now and then. But you could never be a loser, Serena."

His deep voice did something wonderful to her name, giving it an intimacy that made her feel as if she were hearing it for the very first time. When he reached across the small gap between the bucket seats, Serena found herself unable to turn away from the sensual glow in his eyes.

"You really are a remarkably lovely woman." He traced the full curve of her lips with his finger. "I'll admit to being captivated from the beginning, but each time I see you, I find myself discovering another facet of your personality that fascinates me even more."

Serena was trembling under the seduction of his practiced touch. "Alex . . ."

His husky voice sounded as if it were coming from inside a velvet-lined drum. "Just one kiss, Serena. How can that hurt?"

How indeed? she asked herself. Despite the fact that they were sitting in a public parking lot in the middle of the campus, with the bright sun glaring down on them, Serena knew that if she allowed Alex that single kiss he wanted it could prove disastrous.

"I just don't think it's a good idea," she protested softly.

"The trouble with you, Serena, my sweet, is that you think too much."

Before she could discern his intention, Alex's head swooped down and his lips captured hers in a kiss that caused her head to swim. She gripped the steering wheel as the now familiar flood of desire washed over her. The swift, silvery flare ended as abruptly as it began.

Confused, Serena turned on him. "That's not fair!"

He grinned unrepentantly. "Just a friendly kiss to congratulate the victor at the end of a match. It's an old Egyptian custom. Don't tell me you've never heard of it?"

"Of course I haven't. Because it doesn't exist."

"Are you calling me a liar?"

"That's precisely what I'm calling you," Serena responded, shifting the car into gear.

"It's not that different from jumping over the net to shake the winner's hand," he explained patiently.

Serena's only response was to shake her head in mute frustration. They didn't speak for the next few blocks.

"Are you hungry?" Alex asked as she pulled the M.G. into Donovan's driveway.

"Famished."

"Me, too. Want to split a pizza?"

"I can't." Serena denied the offer with obvious reluctance. "I'm in training. Besides," she stated stiffly, "I'm furious at you."

"And well you should be," he agreed. "I behaved outrageously, kissing you against your will like that." He allowed the untruth of Serena's uninvolvement in the kiss to hang in the air between them for a long, wicked moment. "But that's still no reason to forgo lunch. How about my making you a nutritional tuna-fish salad?"

"I don't know." Serena wondered when she had begun to vacillate so badly. Even during those long, depressing days in the hospital, then later the clinic, she had always known precisely where she was going, what she wanted out of life. Since Alex's appearance in her life, she couldn't even make up her mind about tuna fish.

"Go take your shower and change," he suggested. "You'll feel like a new woman." His eyes lit with devilment. "Not that I'm not wild about the one I'm with at the present moment."

Serena got out of the car, too tired to argue any longer. When she reached for the bucket of balls, Alex caught her hand.

"I'll bring those over with lunch."

"I'm not helpless," she flared. "I can certainly manage to carry a stupid plastic bucket filled with tennis balls."

His smile didn't fade in wattage as he lifted her fingers to his lips. "Of course you can," he agreed smoothly. "I was simply attempting to save you some time. Shouldn't you be icing your arm?" His gaze dropped to the long scar running around her forearm.

"I hate it when you're right," she muttered. "Give me thirty minutes, okay?"

"Make it forty-five. You don't want to rush your treatment."

Before she could utter a word of argument, he was out of the car, headed toward his own house, the bucket of balls under his arm. Serena didn't know whether to laugh or cry.

As she applied the ice pack to her arm, Serena tried to discern what it was about Alex that had her so jumpy. He was admittedly friendly, helpful, kind; the man could probably lay claim to at least half the items listed in the Boy Scout creed. Yet she didn't trust him.

While her years of continual travel and dedication to her sport had not allowed an active social life, Serena knew instinctively that Alex Bedare was the type of man who was skilled at turning a woman's head. If they gave out honorary doctoral degrees in such a thing, Alex would undoubtedly be at the head of the line. He was the kind of man who could easily convince a woman to put aside her own goals and dreams while she waited for a single word, a touch, a sign of his approval.

Serena had seen it happen before to women on the tour. Strong, self-sufficient women who allowed themselves to succumb to the loneliness created by the gypsylike existence required from a sport that had no off-season. Lindsay Carlow had been just such a woman. Lindsay had been Serena's doubles partner for six years; together they won consistently, sweeping tournaments all over the world before finally losing a match in Lindsay's native Australia. Accustomed to being the perpetual winner, Lindsay had surprised Serena by crumbling after the match. To this day Serena felt guilty about not talking Lindsay out of her plan to drown her sorrows in one of Melbourne's overly macho pubs.

Lindsay had met a man that night. A strong-bodied, strong-willed man who proclaimed that Lindsay's only problem was that she had been attempting to destroy the natural order of things. Men, he had explained, supplied the strength in the relationship, women the softness. All Lindsay needed was a man to take care of her for a change. In a moment of weakness, aided and abetted by a surfeit of vodka gimlets, Lindsay had decided that was precisely what she needed. Why hadn't she realized all this sooner? Of course it hadn't hurt, Serena considered, still bitter over the way her friend's life had turned out, that the man Lindsay had fallen for possessed thick, sun-gilded hair and dazzling blue eyes. He was, of all things, a lifeguard, possessing the bronze-toned, broad-shouldered body to prove it.

Lindsay had willingly allowed Garrett McDonald to plan her life. When his friends gave him a bad time about his woman making more money than he did, Garret insisted Lindsay quit the tour, which she did. His dislike of her income did not stop him from spending Lindsay's hard-earned funds on beer for his mates, and on a new sailboat. It was several months later, once her money was gone and the novelty of their relationship had worn thin, that Lindsay returned home from her job as a salesgirl in a posh boutique to find Garrett gone. She never saw him again.

Serena could not deny that she'd been happy to learn of their breakup. Shortly after that day, Lindsay had flown to the United States to visit Serena at the clinic. The two women had promised each other that they'd soon be back on top, showing the rest of the tennis world how the game of doubles was meant to be played. That day, which once had seemed doubtful, if not impossible, was no longer so far away. Lindsay had jumped at the chance to pair with Serena in Italy next month.

As Serena tossed the ice bag into the sink, she vowed that she was never going to make the same mistake her friend had. No matter how desperate things might seem, whatever happened at the upcoming charity match, she was going to handle things as she always had. By herself.

Alex's eyes paid compliments as he joined Serena on the wide front porch. "You look gorgeous!"

"Thank you."

"You look great in red. But I suppose you realized that when you bought that blouse."

"I didn't buy it."

"Oh?" he asked carefully. "Since I can't imagine you shoplifting, it must have been a gift from a friend." Alex wondered why that idea should annoy him.

"It was a going-away present from the other patients at the clinic."

He inwardly cringed at the way he blundered into that unhappy topic. "Sorry, I didn't mean to bring up painful memories."

"That's not a painful memory. I made some very good friends there. We were all pulling for one another. Believe it or not, it was a nice feeling. In an odd sort of way."

"They sound like very good friends."

"They were."

"But of course, you undoubtedly liked some better than others."

Serena was finding it increasingly difficult to think with those bright obsidian eyes directed toward her mouth. "I suppose I did."

"Did you have any very close friends, Serena?"

She suddenly understood what he was getting at. "I didn't have an affair, if that's what you mean. Believe it or not, by the time I managed to finish my therapy every day, I was too tired to even think about sex."

"How about now?"

Serena was stunned by Alex's constant seduction ploys. She decided it was simply instinctive behavior. Just as other men breathed without conscious thought, Alex continually cast out sensual lures.

"I thought I was promised lunch."

A ghost of a smile hovered at the corners of his lips. "Don't tell me you're afraid to answer?"

That was getting too close for comfort. "Of course not. But I am starving and if I don't eat something soon, I'll probably swoon right here at your feet. And knowing your one-track mind, you're bound to take it all wrong."

Instead of taking offense, Alex threw back his head and laughed. Then he reached down beside the swing and extracted their lunch from a wicker basket.

"Tuna for iron and protein, cheese for calcium and pasta for carbohydrates," he said as he placed the salad in front of her. "You can't accuse me of not setting a healthy training table."

As she tasted the salad, finding it irritatingly delicious, Serena couldn't ignore the fact that little by little, Alex was infiltrating himself into the smallest pockets of her life, making decisions that were rightfully hers. When Lindsay came to mind, Serena shivered at the unwelcome comparison.

ALEX CONTINUED TO PRACTICE with Serena every day leading up to the charity match. To her surprise, he appeared to have abandoned his sensual campaign, treating her as nothing more than a friend. A pal would have been an even better description, Serena considered one night after returning from horseback riding with him in the foothills north of the campus.

"Nervous?" he asked as they sat out on Donovan's front porch, drinking in the delicious fragrances carried on the gentle breeze.

Serena knew that he was not referring to his close proximity to her on the swing. "Not as much as I was," she admitted. "I suppose I have you to thank for that."

"Me?"

"I don't know what I would have done without you," Serena answered honestly. She granted him a warm smile. "If you decide to change careers again, you might consider coaching tennis."

"I just might, if it meant spending every day with you." Although he returned her smile, Alex's words had an oddly serious tone. One Serena decided not to dwell on for the moment.

"Marty promised he'd be back on his feet for the Italian Open. I hope he's right."

Alex wanted to banish the thoughtful little frown that was threatening to extinguish the light in her eyes. "Surely you can find another coach if he isn't. It seems people would be standing in line to work with you."

"It's not that simple. A working player-coach relationship is about as difficult to find as a good marriage. A good coach must be perceptive and understand a player's moods and feelings."

"And Marty Jennings understands you?" Alex asked, envying the man that ability. Every time he began to get a finger on Serena, she retreated behind her mental barricades, leaving him even more frustrated. She was a puzzle, and one he had every intention of solving.

"As well as anyone can," she said, her answer giving credence to the fact that it was not an easy task. "He's quiet. Mellow. He hardly ever says a word. But he doesn't ever lie to me, either."

"Why would he lie?"

She shrugged. "Oh, to boost my confidence. For example, some coaches might say you're playing well, even if you're not." She frowned. "I've never understood how that's supposed to help. Especially if you're playing sloppily or not giving your best effort."

Alex couldn't imagine Serena ever giving less than her best effort and said so, which encouraged the smile back onto her lips. "I'm probably my hardest critic," she admitted. "That's why I'm grateful that Marty isn't the other kind of coach, either."

"What kind is that?"

"The kind that never gives a player compliments and just stands on the sidelines shoveling criticism, no matter how hard she might be trying. No matter how sick, or tired she is. No matter that she's twisted her knee the day before or has pulled a tendon, or has played for four hours straight with the flu." Serena's voice was strong and furious; she was twisting her hands together in her lap. When she realized Alex was watching her intently, she released a slow, ragged breath that was perilously close to a sob.

"I've never understood the need for negative reinforcement," she finished quietly. "Perhaps some people respond to it. I don't know."

"But you don't."

Serena struggled to find her voice. "No. I don't."

Once again Alex was struck by how fragile Serena could appear when she allowed her vulnerability to show through her sleek veneer. He could picture her as a little girl, long blond braids and wide gray eyes. He had pumped Donovan for information about Serena, learning that she adored hot-fudge sundaes with double nuts, John Wayne Westerns and Siamese cats. Alex knew she had had her tonsils out the summer she was thirteen and had fallen madly in love with a tennis pro at the country club that same year. The pro had not returned her juvenile crush.

He also knew that as a child, Serena had often laid awake long into the night, terrified of falling asleep because of monsters who lurked under her bed and in her closet. It was all Alex could do to keep from pulling her into his arms and promising her that he'd protect her from whatever monsters were lurking out there in the dark. Including those that lingered on from her childhood. Gently, without utilizing force, he untwined Serena's tight fingers. Her short square nails had left gouges on the tops of her hands.

She trembled as his fingertips caressed her skin. Was it desire, he wondered. From his touch? Or perhaps it was something more elemental. Something or someone that might provide the answer to Serena Lawrence.

"What about your father, Serena? Which type of coach was William Lawrence?"

It was a shot in the dark, but he knew he had hit the bull's-eye when she stiffened and her hands went ice cold. She looked away, staring unseeingly into the well of darkness.

"Serena?"

She had gone pale, appearing ashen even in the spreading amber glow of the porch light. "My father was a great tennis player."

"Granted." His fingers circled her wrists. "But that wasn't what I asked you, Serena. And I don't believe the fact that William Lawrence was a champion on the courts is what's making your pulse beat so wildly."

She drew back, all too aware of how helpless she must appear to Alex at this moment. He saw too much with those midnight-black eyes. It was impossible to lie to the man. She might try, but he'd see right through her every time.

The chirp of crickets filled the thick silence. Seeking to banish the pain in those lovely gray eyes, Alex rose to his feet, taking Serena with him.

"I was out of line bringing it up," he said, putting the subject away for now, but vowing that they would discuss it at a more appropriate time. After Serena had regained her confidence. "If we're going to get up in time to practice before my eight o'clock class, I'd better let you get to bed."

He lowered his head and kissed her for the first time in more than two weeks. As she watched Alex cross the yard to his own house, Serena considered that the chaste peck on her forehead had reminded her of something she might expect from her Great-aunt Harriet. Even as she told herself she should be grateful that Alex had obviously moved on to greener sexual pastures, Serena felt herself missing the way he had made her feel, albeit for a short time, like a very desirable woman.

As MUCH AS SHE WOULD HAVE LIKED to forgo the press party the night before the celebrity tournament, Serena realized that it was for a good cause. Besides, she wasn't about to pass up an opportunity to meet Tom Selleck, who had flown in from Hawaii for the occasion.

The television star was in attendance as promised, appearing even more handsome in the flesh. However, with the continual clutch of women gathered around the actor, Serena was forced to settle for observing him from across the room. Not that she would have been given the opportunity to speak with him alone. With wall-to-wall celebrities filling the ballroom of the Los Angeles Biltmore Hotel, Serena was amazed to find herself surrounded by reporters the entire evening.

"How's the injury, Serena?" she was asked by a tall, lanky man from *Sports Illustrated*. When all eyes slid immediately to her arm, Serena was grateful she had possessed the fore-sight to wear a long-sleeved black cocktail dress.

She smiled into the Minicam that suddenly appeared at the outer edges of the circle. "The doctors tell me I'm one hundred percent."

"Even if that's true, will your serve be as strong as ever?" asked a moon-faced young reporter from *Sporting News*.

Again a smile. "I'll be able to answer that better after to-morrow's match."

"Are you saying that you'll base your decision whether or not to return to the tour on your performance tomorrow?" This question came from a bronzed, shapely reporter rep-resenting *Women's Sports*. Serena recognized her as a for-mer Olympic diving champion.

"No, I'm not saying that. I haven't exactly been idle while I've been away. I've been working out, practicing, playing some nontournament games. What I meant was that tomor-row will be the first time I've tried to serve up an ace under pressure."

The woman reporter jumped in to ask a follow-up ques-tion. "The WTA tour doesn't have an off-season. Do you honestly believe you'll be up to the rigors of constant trav-eling after all you've been through?"

Serena's smile didn't waver. "I've never felt better. Men-tally or physically."

"You were on the way to a grand slam before the acci-dent," a reporter from ESPN reminded her needlessly. "Would you like to pull it off this year?"

Stupid question, she thought with a flash of anger. "Cer-tainly, I'd like to win all four of the major tournaments this year." Her smile was growing forced. "Wouldn't everyone?"

There was a murmur of agreement when a short, stocky woman with a cap of flaming orange curls elbowed her way to the front of the group. She shoved a microphone into Ser-ena's face.

"Serena, you've been off the circuit for more than two years. Are you worried about the competition you'll be facing from the younger women?"

Serena's irritation flared even higher, but a lifetime of practice allowed her to conceal it successfully. "I'm only twenty-eight myself," she reminded the reporters quietly.

The woman refused to relinquish the floor. "Are you aware that Gabriella Dupree referred to you as 'over the hill' during the Lakewood Invitational tournament?" A hush settled over this corner of the vast ballroom as everyone awaited Serena's answer.

Watching the clip with Donovan on the eleven o'clock newscast, Alex discerned that to be the precise moment the Ice Princess made her appearance.

"Gabriella is an excellent young competitor," Serena said smoothly. "I'm looking forward to playing her."

Nodding regally to the clutch of reporters, Serena moved fluidly through the crowd, breathing a sigh of relief when she finally escaped to the crisp night air outside the hotel. She was grateful when the limousine driver provided by the tournament appeared to sense her mood, returning her to Claremont in silence.

"You were magnificent!" Donovan greeted her as she arrived back at the house. "You handled those yahoos beautifully."

Serena managed a weak grin of appreciation. "You couldn't tell my smile was frozen onto my face?" She rubbed her jaw. "I think I've abused all my facial muscles beyond redemption."

"You looked beautiful, as ever," Donovan proclaimed loyally. "Even Gloria was transfixed."

"Gloria gave up a rerun of *The Rockford Files* to watch me? How did you talk her into doing that?"

"Your brother wrestled the remote control from her hands." Alex entered the room at that moment, carrying a steaming cup of herbal tea. "Here. Something to soothe your jagged nerves."

Serena accepted the drink gratefully, inhaling the aroma of chamomile and hibiscus flowers, peppermint leaves and cinnamon. "Thank you." She took a sip, finding it delicious, before returning her attention to her brother. "That was a foolish, dangerous thing to do!"

"Hey, I didn't do it alone. Alex helped. In fact, he diverted her attention so I could get hold of the control."

"You did that?" she asked Alex, her eyes widening with a mixture of both surprise and alarm. "Why?"

Alex shrugged. "Neither of us owns a television. We'd planned to watch the news over at one of the dorms, but it turned out that you were competing with *The Bride of Frankenstein* on the movie channel. Gloria was the only person—or ape—we knew who wasn't a horror-film freak."

"It was still a stupid thing to do. You both could have been killed."

Alex grinned. "You're not going to get rid of me that easily, sweetheart. Drink your tea, you look as if you need it. Although after watching those reporters rake you over the coals, I'm tempted to make you a stiff drink."

"I don't drink. As for the reporters, it's their job to ask tactless questions."

"I should have gone with you," Alex ground out.

They had argued about that very fact this afternoon. He had been less than pleased when Serena held firm, insisting that she could handle things by herself. Alex was not accustomed to women continually challenging him at every turn and while he had admittedly admired Serena's independence, he wasn't certain he liked it.

Serena sipped her tea, experiencing a relaxing warmth. "We've gone over this a hundred times," she complained. "I didn't want to explain our relationship to that mob. They'd be bound to get the wrong idea."

He shot her a cool, dangerous look. "Or the right one." Before she could challenge that statement, he continued. "Anyway, the fact remains that you shouldn't have to face things like that alone."

At his gruff tone, Serena eyed him curiously over the rim of her cup. "I'm used to it."

He waved away her response. "That has nothing to do with it, Serena. You were thrown into a den of hungry lions tonight and I'm never going to forgive myself for allowing that to happen."

Serena's mouth dropped open. "You? Allow?" Her voice rose high enough to shatter glass. "Just what gives you any right to talk to me that way?"

Alex rose to his full height and glared down at her, his black eyes flashing dangerously. "I care about you, damn it! And it's not my fault if you're either too blind or too stupid to see that."

Her temper rising to the boiling point, Serena looked inclined to swing at Alex when Donovan stepped into the breach. "Alex really was concerned about your welfare, runt. I practically had to tie him down when they brought up Gabriella."

"Gabriella." Serena's tone was edged with frost. "If that woman spent half as much time practicing her ground strokes as she does putting on her makeup, she might be capable— just barely—of giving me a decent match."

Donovan laughed as he put his arm around Serena and pulled her to him for a brotherly hug. "I'm glad to see you haven't lost your spunk, sweetheart."

She finished off her tea. "Never. I was the best in the sport three years ago and I have every intention of working my way back to the top. One tournament at a time. My only hope is that during one of them, I beat those ridiculous ruffled panties off Gabriella Dupree."

Serena handed Alex her empty cup. "I appreciate your support," she said with a vast display of outward calm. "And I apologize for yelling at you. Now, if you gentlemen will excuse me, I think I'll go upstairs to bed. I have a big day ahead of me tomorrow."

Two pairs of male eyes watched her leave the room. Donovan's green ones reflected brotherly love while Alex's black eyes glittered with overt frustration. He expelled a weary sigh.

"I'm beginning to understand why she feels the need to do it, but I could sure learn to hate your sister when she pulls that Ice Princess routine."

Donovan laughed appreciatively. His expression instantly sobered as he took in the stormy torment in Alex's dark gaze. "Give her some time. The past few years have been tough on her. And she's not used to sharing her feelings at the best of times." He lifted his glass in salute. "But if anyone can melt that glacier, Alex, my friend, I believe you're just the man to pull it off."

Encouraged slightly by Donovan's appraisal of the situation, Alex managed a crooked grin. "I'm sure as hell going to give it the old college try."

6

SERENA'S RETURN to the world of tennis the following day could have been choreographed by the Keystone Cops. It began innocently enough, when she arrived at the courts, pleased to find herself paired with the handsome star of a popular television-detective series.

Eat your heart out, Gloria, she thought as she was introduced to the actor. Easily deflecting his prematch passes, Serena enjoyed the casual flirting. The light bantering was far less threatening than the conversations she had experienced with Alex.

Unfortunately, Serena was soon to discover that the man looked a great deal better than he played. She was accustomed to giving up more of the court to her male partner when playing mixed doubles and, under normal conditions, usually allowed the man to field the questionable down-the-middle shots. That was not to be the case today.

She was forced to skid to more than one abrupt, dangerous stop when her partner suddenly stepped in front of her to return a ball that was rightfully hers. During other volleys he was just as likely to let the ball bounce, then give her a puzzled look when she didn't rush in to return it. In the first game of the second set, she nearly fell while scrambling to avoid being decapitated when the actor swung wildly at an easy crosscourt lob that should have been hers. In spite of his erratic style of play, Serena had to admit the man was not without his charms. His apologetic, boyish grin promptly melted her flash of irritation every time.

Despite their comedy of errors, Serena and the actor won the match, overcoming the effort put forth by an aging, overweight comedian and a buxom young starlet 7-5, 6-3. Serena's partner, behaving as if he had never possessed a single doubt as to the outcome, gave her an exuberant kiss, to the delight of the reporters covering the event. She could hear the motor drives of the Nikons whirring away as the photographers captured the kiss for their various publications. After shaking hands with their vanquished opponents, Serena glanced up at the grandstand, her eyes locking with Alex's intense black ones. Her pulse soared.

As his gaze swept over her uplifted face, Alex found himself struggling with an alien, distracting feeling he unwillingly recognized as jealousy. It had taken all the self-restraint he possessed not to jump over the railing and charge out on the court, knocking that handsome actor onto the seat of his tight white shorts when he had covered Serena's soft, pliant mouth with that kiss. It didn't matter that the kiss was more for show—a staged media event guaranteed to make the papers—than seduction. Alex knew all too well that kissing Serena Lawrence could easily become a habit. Wasn't he suffering from the same addiction himself? He was damned if he wanted some hotshot television star to home in on his woman.

His woman. Wouldn't Serena explode if she knew he had come to think of her that way? The idea made him want to smile. The only time she dropped her air of cool composure, other than the few kisses they had shared, was when her temper flared. It was almost enough to tempt a man to keep her furious all the time. Except in bed. Then he would want her warm and willing, alive with all of the passion but none of the anger. God, how he wanted her! His entire being ached with hunger for Serena.

She was never out of his mind, appearing to him in a myriad of sensual poses, enticing places. While his conscious mind had been well aware of every move she was making on the red-clay court, including the time that idiot almost took her head off with his racket, Alex's subconscious mind had peeled away the tailored, unadorned tennis dress, allowing him to picture her nude, her long golden legs flashing in the dappled afternoon sunlight.

Serena was possessed with an innate, balletic grace, but she was more than graceful. She was the most fluid player he had ever seen; she reminded him of a sleek cat. Exceptionally quick, she covered the court with uncanny anticipation, seeming to know where the ball was going before it left her opponent's racket. She was beauty and grace personified. And she was driving him up a wall.

Serena's smile did not fade as she posed for the cameras, but her mind was paralyzed from the impact of Alex's blazing dark eyes. They kindled an awareness deep inside her, a warmth that surged through her veins, melting her bones until she was not sure she could continue to stand unassisted. She managed to answer the questions thrown at her by the press instinctively, automatically, relieved when she had finally escaped to the locker room.

Standing under the shower, she tilted her head back, allowing the cool water to sluice over her, willing it to dampen her desire for a man she had no business thinking about. Even if she had room for a man in her life—which she didn't, Serena reminded herself firmly—never in a million years would she choose Alex Bedare to be that man. Oh, she had no doubt he'd be an exceptional lover—skilled, considerate, adept at pleasuring a woman. But he would also insist on total surrender, something Serena had absolutely no intention of giving to any man. Even one who could make her pulse jump with a single glance, her heart turn somersaults with the most casual of touches.

"No," she muttered. "No, no, no!"

"Awfully negative thoughts from a lady who just played as if she'd never been away." The feminine voice was laced with both affection and laughter, the Australian singsong accent sounding like a composite of English and Texan.

Serena's eyes flew open. "Lindsay!" Unthinkingly she flung her arms around her old friend. A moment later she backed away. "I've soaked you through to the skin."

Lindsay shrugged nonchalantly. "What's a little water between friends? Besides, it's nice to see that you haven't lost your enthusiasm, love. Wouldn't do to have me doubles partner in anything less than full form when we play together in Italy next month." Her brown eyes danced with anticipation.

"It's so good to see you!" Serena grabbed a folded towel from the stack on a nearby bench and wrapped it around herself. "Have you been here long?"

"Long enough to watch you and the hunk clean up out there. I've got just one question."

Serena rubbed her hair dry with another towel. "Shoot."

Lindsay grinned wickedly. "'Ow in the bloody hell could you keep your mind on your game with those tight buns running back and forth in front of you?"

Serena laughed. Lindsay had always been good for her, reminding her not to take life so seriously. Despite her high ranking, Lindsay played as hard off the court as she did on. In a way, Serena had always envied her friend that ability. That was another reason she had been so distressed when Lindsay had almost thrown her life away on that lifeguard, but from the impish gleam in Lindsay's brown eyes, Serena realized her former partner had her life back on track.

"I didn't notice," she said, bending down to dry her legs.

"Liar. The man was absolutely gorgeous, every suntanned inch of him. From the top of 'is gilt-blond hair right down to 'is feet. And those eyes." She sighed dramatically.

"When he doffed his sunglasses to smile into the television news cameras, I thought I'd faint dead away on the spot."

"I don't remember you being a swooner."

"And I don't remember *you* being blind, love," Lindsay countered. She chewed thoughtfully on a peach-tinted fingernail as Serena blew her hair dry. "Or perhaps it's simply that you have your mind on other things. Such as that sexy sheikh in the front row."

"I don't know who you're talking about." Serena buttoned her emerald-green silk blouse and tucked it into a softly flared matching skirt.

"Don't pull that Ice Princess act with me, dearie. We go back too far," her friend said, crossing her arms as she leaned back against the wall. "You know very well who I'm talking about. The bloke whose midnight eyes were eating you up the entire match."

Serena fastened a slender gold chain around her wrist. A pair of small gold hoop earrings were her only other jewelry. "You always have possessed an overly active imagination." Her smile was bright, professional and entirely false. "Ready to go share in the celebration festivities?"

Lindsay's frustrated sigh ruffled her nut-brown bangs. "Since I can't pry any intimate little secrets out of you today, we might as well. Will I get to meet the hunk?"

"I'll introduce you to him personally," Serena promised. "From then on, it's up to you."

Lindsay flicked her hair back over her shoulder. "Piece of cake," she said as she snapped her fingers.

Serena had half expected to find Alex waiting for her outside the locker room. When he wasn't there, she decided he must have gone on to the party. She knew he had an invitation. Donovan, who had managed to show up just in time for the first set, had begged off attending the party. He wanted to conduct dream experiments on Gloria in an attempt to get to the bottom of her insomnia problem.

Personally Serena thought an overdose of *Miami Vice* and *Riptide* was leaving Gloria overexcited by bedtime. She had related her theory to Donovan, suggesting reruns of *Leave it to Beaver* or *The Brady Bunch*. At any rate, Donovan had offered his invitation to Alex, who had wasted no time in accepting.

Serena was puzzled and more than a little irritated when he wasn't at the party, either. The least he could have done, she considered furiously, was to stick around long enough to offer congratulations. While the competition had certainly not been what she would soon be facing on the professional tour, she had played well. Her ground strokes had been strong, her lobs well placed. And her serve had shown not a single sign of weakness. In fact, she had made three aces. Surely that deserved some recognition.

She wandered aimlessly through the crowd, answering the same questions about her arm, her future and Gabriella Dupree over and over again until she thought she'd scream. Finally, deciding that she had put in enough time for charity, Serena waved goodbye to Lindsay, who was happily chatting with "the hunk," and left.

The house was dark when Serena arrived home, evidence that Donovan did indeed intend to sit up all night with Gloria. Used to her brother's obsessive work habits, Serena was not surprised, but she would have welcomed a little company. Despite her victory today, despite Lindsay's appearance at the match, she found herself feeling slightly depressed. And she was more than a little concerned about the upcoming Italian tournament in spite of the assured image she projected to the rest of the world.

Serena couldn't help casting a speculative glance toward the house next door, where an amber light glowed through the stained-glass window. Before she could decide whether or not her behavior was prudent, she was marching across the ivy separating the two houses.

Alex greeted her with a bland, unrevealing expression. "Well, this is a nice surprise."

"Where were you?" Serena demanded, brushing past him into the house without waiting for an invitation.

His lips quirked under his mustache as he closed the door and followed her into a small, octagon-shaped parlor. In deference to the cool California night, he had lit a fire.

"Could I offer you something to drink? Juice? Tea? Perhaps a cup of hot chocolate?"

Serena, who had been prepared to refuse anything Alex had to offer, found herself weakening. "With marshmallows?"

"Of course."

"All right," she agreed. "That sounds nice. But first I want to know where you were tonight." Unconsciously her hands curled into fists at her hips.

Lord, she was beautiful, Alex thought, eyeing the sparks emanating from her. Steeped in her own exasperation, Serena failed to notice his appreciative study.

He held out his hands. "Right here. Where did you think I'd be?"

"I thought you'd be at the party." Damn. She sounded just like a petulant child.

"I see."

Serena's blond hair held gleaming highlights from the flickering glow given off by the fire. "No," she insisted firmly. "I don't believe you do."

I know more than you'd like me to, he argued silently. *I know that you're having as difficult a time staying away from me as I am keeping away from you.*

"Come explain while I fix the hot chocolate," he suggested easily.

She followed him into the kitchen and perched stiffly on a stool at the counter. "Donovan said he'd given you his invitation."

Alex took a carton of milk from the refrigerator. "He did." He put the carton on the counter and reached into the lower cupboard for a saucepan.

Serena cleared her throat. "So why didn't you come?"

He poured the milk into the pan and turned on the burner. The blue flame came immediately to life, licking at the copper bottom of the pan. "I didn't think you'd miss me." His tone was mild.

Serena twisted her hands together in her lap. "Well, I did."

There. She'd said it. The unwilling admission had been a rash act, a reckless one. But she would do it again in a minute.

Alex turned slowly. He could handle her cool restraint, although he admittedly found it to be hellishly irritating; he found her bursts of anger exciting. To be honest, he had baited her on more than one occasion in order to watch her temper flare. Underneath that icy exterior, Serena was all fire.

However, at the moment, viewing the uncertainty in her wide gray eyes, his hunger for her was overcome by a stronger feeling of tenderness. How strange that it should be her softness that proved his downfall, Alex considered. He found her unexpected vulnerability impossible to resist.

He ran a finger lightly over the slope of her shoulder. It had not escaped his attention that Serena favored bright, vibrant clothing. Exciting shades. He wondered if she even realized her behavior was an act of unconscious rebellion against the life she'd lived for so many years.

"Did I tell you that you were magnificent today?"

"No." It was a whisper, but easily heard in the stillness of the night.

"You were. I've never seen anything as exciting as the way you moved around that court." His hand cupped the back of her neck while his thumb stroked her throat. "Do you know what I was thinking?"

Something rippled along her skin, something alien, exciting. Frightening. Serena shook her head, suddenly mute.

When his lips replaced his thumb, Serena drew in a quick, harsh breath. "I was imagining what you'd look like without that virginal white tennis dress on," he admitted, his words a warm breeze as he bit down gently on her earlobe. "I was envisioning making love to you all day, all night, on and on, forever. Until you could think of only one thing. Me."

Alex combed his fingers through her hair, tilting her head so her eyes met his. "Only me."

She was trembling as he gently pulled her off the stool, bringing her into his arms. "That would prove a bit distracting," she managed to say, even as her hands curled around his neck. Desire rose, ripe and hot.

His lips moved over her cheek, loitering at her temple, leaving sparks wherever they touched. "That's the idea."

Serena closed her eyes to the waves of golden light flooding through her body. If only it were possible. If only she could give herself up to the pleasure she knew Alex would bring to their lovemaking. But it was too true: he had been nothing but a distraction from the moment she met him. She had worked too hard, too long, to turn back now. Every instinct Serena possessed told her that if she succumbed to Alex's enticing invitation, the past two and a half years would be for nothing.

His hands moved down her back, caressing her with a confident, practiced touch. "I like this blouse," he murmured. His palms traced lazy circles up and down her spine, soothing gestures that excited rather than calmed. "It makes me want to touch you, to discover if you're as soft as I've imagined. As soft as this silk," Serena found herself unable to resist as he tugged the material free of her waistband.

His fingers slipped under the spun silk. "Ah," he breathed. "I knew it. Rose petals, butterfly wings, snowflakes—none of them even come close."

Serena's bones liquefied under his scorching touch. He had lured her to the very brink of sanity, and she knew it would only take the gentlest of shoves before she went tumbling over the edge. She forced herself to think of her career, to concentrate on her future, instead of this one shimmering, ethereal moment. As William Lawrence's composed aristocratic features swam into view, Serena found the strength to resist.

She rested her forehead against his shoulder and shook her head. "No."

Alex's fingers spanned her rib cage. "You don't mean that." His voice was low, rough. But his hands remained blissfully gentle, warming her flesh under their beguiling, persuasive touch.

When she lifted her head, Serena's eyes held a soft sheen of moisture. "I do," she whispered.

Her hands, which should have been pushing him away, refused to obey her mental commands. Instead they seemed to have developed minds of their own as her fingers curved into his shoulders. Strong shoulders, they would be capable of carrying broad burdens. She ran her hands down his arms. A woman could feel safe in these arms. Protected. Even treasured. Serena shook her head, reminding herself that she was not seeking protection, nor did she wish to be any man's personal treasure.

"No," she repeated, more firmly this time.

Alex cupped her chin in his fingers, his thumb lightly teasing her bottom lip. Walls. Serena had surrounded herself with protective barriers that had taken a lifetime to erect. It would be the height of conceit, even for him, to think he could scale those parapets in less than three weeks. He would have to give her more time.

While his years in the diplomatic corps had taught Alex patience, such behavior ran against the natural grain of his temperament. His father had often chided him gently for his impatient streak, declaring it to be an American trait inherited from his mother. Perhaps. All Alex knew at this moment was that waiting for Serena would be one of the most difficult tasks he had ever faced.

"The milk is burning," he said with a sigh, recognizing the harsh odor. Unwillingly he released her.

Serena's hands dropped to her sides. "That's all right. I have to be going home."

His eyes were laced with gentle affection. "Without sampling my gourmet hot chocolate?"

"It's fattening anyway. I'm in training."

Something in her tone tugged at him, encouraging feelings of protectiveness to flow over his lingering desire. She was so powerful on the court, so cool in life, so very independent, it was easy to forget how small she was. How human. Alex knew something was bothering her. Something that went beyond her desire to avoid personal involvement with him. His palms sloped her shoulders, easing out the renewed tension he felt there.

Suddenly nervous, Serena's eyes darted past Alex toward the stove. "Your milk really is burning," she offered, struggling to achieve a firmer emotional footing. Once again Alex had made her feel uncertain, uneasy.

"Forget the milk." His hands slid down her arms, his fingers circling her wrists. He could feel the increased beat of her blood. "Why did you come here tonight, Serena?" he asked quietly.

Her slender shoulders lifted in a half shrug. "I didn't have any particular reason. It was just an impulse. I was still a little up from the tournament and didn't feel like going to bed quite yet."

His somber gaze plumbed the soft gray depths of her eyes. She was lying. But instinct told him not to push. She'd tell him in her own time; he'd see to that.

"Go in the other room and enjoy the fire," he suggested. "I'll heat a fresh pan of milk and be right in."

As gratitude flooded into her eyes, Alex was hit with a staggering emotion far stronger than the impatience or even the hunger Serena had instilled in him from the beginning. Shaken, he stared after her. Then, unable or unwilling to examine the cause of the discomforting feeling, he turned away and dumped the scalded milk down the drain.

7

ALEX PAUSED IN THE DOORWAY, drinking in the alluring vision of Serena seated on the midnight-blue Persian rug in front of the fireplace, her legs tucked under her. She was staring into the flickering gold and orange flames, but her thoughts were obviously elsewhere. Alex felt that now familiar but still undefined pain deep in his chest.

"Hot chocolate with marshmallows," he said cheerily as he entered the cozy room. "Just what the lady ordered."

Serena glanced up. "You make me nervous when you suddenly turn considerate."

"Suddenly? I thought it was my usual behavior." He gave her an easy, amiable grin as he dropped down beside her on the rug.

Serena laughed lightly at that. "Your *usual* behavior is to be argumentative, dictatorial and maddeningly chauvinistic."

He tugged on the ends of her sleek hair. "Chauvinistic? Me?"

Shaking her head free of his fingers, Serena chased a plump marshmallow around the mug. Alex had to bite back his groan when she licked the chocolate from her top lip.

"Chauvinistic," she repeated decisively. "Any woman would have to be crazy to get mixed up with a man like you. Still, if even half of what my brother tells me is true, an amazing number of women have foolishly tempted fate."

"Is that what you consider our relationship? Tempting fate?"

Serena didn't answer immediately. Instead, she returned her gaze to the fire as she sipped the hot chocolate. When she turned back to him, her eyes were suddenly serious.

"I suppose I do."

Serena didn't resist as Alex took her hand. His thumb grazed over her knuckles. "I probably shouldn't ask this next question."

"That's right," she agreed shakily. It was impossible to misread the gleam in his eyes. "You shouldn't."

Alex lifted her hand to his lips and feathered a kiss against her skin. Serena felt the jolt all the way to her toes. He held her gaze over their linked hands. "Fools rush in . . ."

Alex's eyes didn't release hers as he put his mug down on the stone hearth. With his free hand, he stroked her hair, enjoying the soft, luxurious feel of it against his palm.

"Are you tempted, Serena?"

There was nothing to be gained by lying. Serena had come to the conclusion that she could hide nothing from this man. She exhaled a soft, rippling sigh. "Yes," she said quietly. "Yes, I'm afraid I am."

His palm moved to her cheek. "Afraid?"

As he leaned toward her, Serena unconsciously parted her lips. Alex knew she would accept his kiss. But he was discovering that he was a selfish man. He wanted it all. It would not be enough that Serena would merely permit him to make love to her. He wanted her to be as desperate, as hungry for it as he was.

Patience. Alex reminded himself of his father's frequent admonition. He could be as patient as hell, if that was what it would take to unleash the vast store of passion he knew flowed through Serena's blue blood. Donovan had told him a bit about her heritage and for a fleeting moment he damned that icy British restraint she had obviously learned from her father, the tennis-playing viscount. Alex immediately reconsidered that idea. Without that frustrating reserve, would

Serena be so tantalizing? So exciting? The flash and heat of
a steaming volcano wrapped in the icy sleet of a blizzard
That was Serena Lawrence.

Serena watched, mesmerized by the range of emotions
moving over Alex's face. Desire, lust, anger, resolve. All in
a few fleeting seconds. He was as changeable as the weather
sultry warmth one moment, violent storms the next. That
alone should have warned her away. Serena wanted—no she
needed—some semblance of predictability in her life. Alex
would never give her that. Passion, yes. Exhilaration, yes
Even tenderness. But predictability? She might as well ask for
the moon. Serena shook her head to clear her thoughts as she
realized Alex had asked her a question.

"I asked why you were afraid of me," he repeated. His voice
was low, calm, but she could hear the intensity shrouded just
below the surface.

Serena unconsciously covered his hand with hers. "Not of
you," she corrected. "Of us."

His lips curled in a smile. "At least now you're willing to
admit that there is an *us*."

Self-satisfaction practically oozed from his every male
pore, reminding Serena that to Alex, this was all a game. One
he played very skillfully. She jerked her hand away. After
placing her mug beside his on the hearth, Serena drew her
knees to her chest and wrapped her arms around them in an
unconscious gesture of protection.

"You're misinterpreting my words again," she answered
coolly. "I meant to say that I find our situation nerve
racking."

Patience. Anger rocketed through him, making him want
to shake her until she would at least admit that the feelings
that had been driving him mad these past weeks were not his
alone. Alex took a deep breath, reminding himself that no
negotiating session had ever been won by a reckless display
of temper. His fingers gripped the mug as he tossed his head

back and swallowed quickly, wishing it contained something stronger than cocoa.

Serena stared, both frightened and fascinated at the same time. "And I thought I'd learned to control my temper," she murmured.

His expression gave nothing away. It was smooth, polite, even distant. But a storm continued to swirl in his eyes. "Occupational necessity."

She nodded. "We have that in common."

"Yes. I suppose we do," Alex agreed in a deceptively mild tone. He reached out, moving his hand down her throat. Her quickened pulse resembled the frantic fluttering of a hummingbird's wings. "You want me," he insisted.

"Yes," she whispered. As his head ducked down, Serena hastened to qualify her answer. "But I don't *want* to want you."

She had barely gotten the words out when his lips fused to hers, warm and demanding, tearing at foundations that were already crumbling down around her. Swept with an uncontrollable desperation, she avidly returned his kisses and when that was no longer enough, she flung her arms around his neck, pulling him close, burying her lips into the warm flesh above his collar.

She didn't utter a word of protest as Alex slowly lowered her to the rug. Her head spun with conflicting messages as she willingly accepted his strength, bending before his power like a willow in the wind. She welcomed the blinding urgency of his lips; she absorbed his passion through each and every one of her body's cells until she felt that she would soon explode from the escalating heat.

Behind her closed lids, sparks burst forth as if from the fire, soaring into the heavens where they erupted into a shimmering display of brilliant light. Alex's lips moved to her ear to murmur deep, vibrating words whose meaning transcended any need for translation. Serena trembled in his arms, twisting her head in an attempt to recapture those strong, wonderful lips.

As Alex slipped his hands under her blouse, her skin felt like liquid satin to the touch. Serena's body was firmer than those of the women he was accustomed to. But as she moved fluidly under his caresses, he discovered that, despite her strength, she was soft. Luxuriously, enticingly soft. Her breasts, while not voluptuous, swelled to fit his hand with such perfection that it crossed his turmoiled mind that she could have been created specifically for his touch. Her long legs were tangled with his, but as his fingers slid up her thigh, Serena covered his hands with her own.

"I can't," she protested softly.

Alex braced himself on his forearms and stared down into her love-softened features. "Can't? Or won't?"

Defensive, Serena struggled for a lingering thread of control. "Does it matter?" she managed to ask, even as she was turning to jelly under his dark gaze.

Alex was forced to watch helplessly as Serena began encasing herself in enough ice to create a new continent. A stream of violent curses went through his mind. As fluent in his mother's native English as he was his father's Arabic, Alex also spoke German, Hebrew, French, a smattering of Greek and enough Russian to get himself arrested. But even with all those languages at his fingertips, he could think of no words harsh enough to express the frustration he felt at this moment.

"Probably not," he answered her finally.

He suddenly sat up and stared blackly into the fire. Serena observed him warily, intrigued by the muscle jerking in his rigid jaw. When he turned to her, his smile held a dangerous, biting challenge.

"We're going to make love, Serena. Sooner or later."

Serena sat up as well, her back straight, her chin directed his way. "You sound very sure of yourself." There was more than a touch of haughtiness in her tone.

She was driving him insane, but Alex had to admire her style. He knew her heart had to be pounding as harshly as his, her mind still fogged by lingering vestiges of desire. But damned if she didn't remind him of some deposed Russian empress.

He experienced some small measure of satisfaction when he reached out and trailed his fingers lazily over her breasts, lingering just long enough to feel the heat generated through the emerald silk. While her mind might still object, her body was instinctively responding to his touch.

"I'm going to touch you," he promised softly, decisively. "First I'm going to undress you slowly, unwrapping these cruel layers of clothing between us one piece at a time. Then my hands are going to touch you, inch by glorious, satiny inch, here...and there...and there as well," he said, his eyes moving over her slender body with the impact of a physical caress.

Serena found herself unable to break away from his heated gaze, unable to resist the sensual scene he was painting with his arousing words.

Alex's black eyes glittered, pupils and irises merging to gleaming obsidian. Serena could view the flames of the fire reflected in those hypnotizing eyes.

"Yes," he insisted, his hands following the trail his gaze had forged, moving freely, possessively over her. "Then, when I've discovered every sensitive, secret place, every flash point, I'm going to kiss each one until your flesh is burning from the feel of my lips."

Serena struggled against the rising tide of desire, fighting the way her rebellious body was softening instinctively at his low, seductive voice.

"When you're crying out, begging me to take you, I'm going to enter you slowly, drawing every bit of bottled-up passion from you until neither of us can hold back another moment."

He fused his mouth against hers, the kiss hard, quick. "And then, when we've both been to heaven and back, you'll be mine, Serena Lawrence. Mine and mine alone."

His possessive tone sent a chill down her spine, where moments before sparks had played. "I won't belong to any man," she insisted, her voice a ragged thread of sound.

Patience. Alex smothered the hunger that lingered, hot and insistent. His answering smile was bold, rakish, vanishing so quickly Serena thought she might have imagined it.

"That's where you're wrong, sweetheart," he said. "Because you will. As I'll belong to you. Whether you like it or not, neither of us has had any choice from the beginning."

"I can't deal with this," Serena protested shakily. "Not now. Not at this point in my life."

Alex forced a shrug. "I'll accept that." When her answering expression revealed her surprise, he ran his finger down her cheek. "For now. I'm not a patient man, Serena, but I suppose I can wait for you to admit the inevitability of our affair until I return from Washington."

"You're going away?"

There it was again. Alex wondered why he had never realized he was such a sucker for vulnerability. He seemed unable to muster up a single defense against it.

His hands were far from steady as he brushed Serena's bangs off her forehead and pressed a reassuring kiss against her temple. "I'll only be gone four or five days. I have a conference in Washington beginning the day after tomorrow. I leave in the morning."

Serena's heart sank. How strange that she should take his leaving so hard. After all, she was scheduled to go to Italy in just a few days herself.

"I won't be here when you get back," she said quietly.

Alex put his arm around her shoulder. "I know. Rome." His squeeze was gentle. "You'll have a wonderful time; it's one of my favorite cities."

Serena leaned her head against his shoulder. "I suppose you've been there."

"A few times. Six or seven, I suppose. You lose track after a while." His fingers played with the ends of her hair where they curved around her chin.

Serena sighed. "I know the feeling. Except I usually just end up seeing the airports. Sight-seeing takes too much time and energy away from my game."

Deciding this was not the time to point out that Serena had a definite problem with priorities, Alex wisely held his tongue. They remained that way for a while, the mood relaxed, as they enjoyed the rich aroma of the burning cedar, the crackling of the bright orange fire.

"Want to tell me about it?" he asked, his lips against her forehead.

Serena continued to stare into the dancing flames. "What?"

He lifted a smooth curtain of hair from the nape of her neck, breathing in a soft scent he knew owed nothing to expensive French perfume.

"What really brought you here tonight? Besides the fact that you can't keep your hands off my body."

His teasing smile meant no offense. Serena took none. "I needed to talk to someone," she admitted reluctantly.

He linked their fingers together. "There's always Donovan."

She shook her head. "He's spending the night with Gloria. Besides, I can't trust him to be honest."

Alex frowned, puzzled. "Your brother wouldn't lie to you. He loves you too much."

"That's just the point." She let out an unsteady breath. "I need someone who can be objective. Someone who'll tell me the truth, even if it might hurt." A single tear escaped, appearing like a brilliant diamond on her cheek.

Alex released her hand to brush the moisture away with his knuckles. *What makes you think I can be objective when it comes to you, Serena Lawrence?* he asked her silently.

"You're afraid of the trip to Italy," he guessed correctly.

When she didn't answer immediately, he took hold of her chin, directing her shielded gaze his way. "While the male population of Rome readily appreciates a lovely woman, I think the practice of kidnapping a bride has gone out of fashion in recent years." His grin encouraged an answering one in return. "Although, I'll have to admit, one look at you would probably make more than one red-blooded Italian male reconsider the idea."

Serena managed a crooked half smile. Alex was good for her when he wasn't coming on like some cross between Don Juan and Genghis Khan. He knew how to make her smile. He knew the things to say that could encourage a laugh. How long had it been since she had relaxed enough to simply enjoy the moment? Too long, she thought.

"I'm afraid of how I'll do," she admitted reluctantly.

His gaze dropped to her arm. The scar was covered by the green sleeve of her blouse. "You didn't display any signs of weakness today. Not that I could see."

"It was only a doubles match, Alex. A celebrity doubles match," she stressed. "The single challenging thing about the entire event was trying to keep out of the way of flying rackets. That guy may be a hotshot television star, but he should definitely stay off tennis courts if he wants to maintain his macho, he-man image."

"Funny you should bring that up," Alex said offhandedly. "Did I ever tell you about the study published in last month's *New England Journal of Medicine*?"

"What study?" she asked suspiciously, prewarned by the devils dancing in his eyes.

"The one comparing control on the tennis court with control in the bedroom. Researchers have proven that the two are definitely linked."

Serena laughed, as she was supposed to. "You are the most outrageous liar I've ever met."

He traced her upturned lips with the tip of his index finger. "It's true," he protested, his own grin threatening to break through at any moment. "And if you'll recall, sweetheart, I'm magnificent on the tennis court."

Serena reached up to brush back a lock of ebony hair, which had fallen over his forehead. "Ah, but you're only ranked twenty-second," she pointed out. "I'm sorry, Alex, but I've always believed in going first class."

She shrieked as Alex pressed her quickly, firmly onto her back. When he covered her wiggling body with his own, Serena experienced a renewed stirring of desire.

"You want first class?" he asked, punctuating his words with sharp, stinging little kisses.

"Yes. No. Oh, damn it, Alex," she complained, pushing against his shoulders, "you promised to give me time. I don't consider five minutes a fair trial period!"

He sighed dramatically. "Probably not." His softened gaze moved over her face. "You know, I think the Mideast peace talks were easier to negotiate than this relationship."

"It wouldn't be so difficult if you wouldn't keep getting off the track," she replied.

"Ah, but I wouldn't keep getting off the track if you weren't so sexy," he countered as he reluctantly rolled off her. He lay on his back, his head pillowed by his arms, his eyes closed. "You are quite honestly driving me crazy, Serena Lawrence."

It was no more than what he was doing to her, Serena could have answered. "Sorry."

One brilliant ebony eye popped open. "Sorry enough to change your mind?"

Serena grabbed a pillow from the sofa and threw it at his head. "Wretch. You almost had me feeling sorry for you."

"It was worth a try," he grumbled.

The laughter died in his eyes, to be replaced by a tenderness Serena found far more threatening than his earlier desire. She felt herself beginning to tremble once again as he reached out to gently stroke her arm.

"Let me see."

Unable to resist his softly issued request, Serena pushed up her sleeve. Alex studied her arm in the glow of the firelight, his fingers tracing the white scar.

"Does it hurt?"

"No more than usual."

His eyes narrowed. "That wasn't what I asked."

"A little."

"Does it hurt more than it did before today's match?"

"Not now." At his questioning gaze, Serena elaborated. "It was a little sore immediately after the match. I put some ice on it. That usually helps."

"Yes," he murmured thoughtfully. "It would." When he pressed his lips to the thin white line, Serena felt as if he touched a sparkler to her skin.

His hand moved up her arm, his fingers pressing into her biceps. "For someone so slender, you're amazingly strong. Do you lift weights?"

She nodded. "And swim. As well as agility drills, springs and rope jumps."

When did she have time for pleasure, he wondered. Did Serena even know what it was to spend a lazy Sunday in bed with a pot of coffee, some freshly baked croissants, a thick newspaper and someone whose company you enjoyed? Did she ever take off from her grueling schedule for long, romantic walks in the rain, drives in the country, lovemaking in front of a fragrant fire in some remote, snowbound cabin?

Alex promised himself that, if nothing else, he would teach Serena the enjoyment life had to offer. He was a proponent of hard work; before he had resigned to take this teaching post, his career had often been described as meteoric. But as hard as Alex labored, he had always played with equal fervor.

His brows drew together. "What, no daily jogs of ten or twelve miles?"

Serena missed the slight tinge of sarcasm sharpening his tone. "Jogging shortens your muscles; I keep it down to a couple of miles every three days. I do a lot of wind sprints, though. They're good for speed and stamina."

"Did you train this rigorously before your injury?"

"I've always trained hard. My father said it was the mark of a champion."

"Or the curse of one," he muttered.

"Excuse me?" she inquired stiffly.

"Knock off the Mrs. Astor routine, duchess," he returned, rapidly losing patience. "If you spent half as much time learning how to be a human being as you do working on that stupid game, you might discover that you're a flesh-and-blood woman. Instead of a confused mass of nerves."

Stunned by his accusation, Serena jumped to her feet. "That's a horrible thing to say!" A lump rose in her throat as she stared down at him. At this moment, Serena didn't know which she wanted to do more, start throwing things at him or turn and run away.

Alex rose wearily from the rug. "See," he said, gripping her shoulders. "You're on the verge of crying, but you can't decide whether they're going to be tears of anger or of wounded pride. Face it, Serena, you can't make up your mind how you feel about us because at this point in your life, you're afraid to discover what you feel about anything. Anyone. It's easier to keep your head in the sand, isn't it? That way you won't have to see that the world isn't the perfect, polite place your daddy told you it would be."

Serena tried to shake loose, but his fingers only tightened. "I wish I'd never met you," she flared. "You're egotistical, arrogant, insufferable . . ."

"And right," he concluded as she paused to take a breath. "Don't forget that one, Serena, because it's the most important of the lot."

She flung her head back. Her eyes shot furious sparks. "You're not right about this!"

Alex's face was inches from hers, his dark eyes dangerous whirlpools. "Oh, no?" he shot back. "Then tell me the last time you played."

"This afternoon. Or is your memory so poor you've already forgotten I helped earn over a hundred thousand dollars for charity today?"

Alex released her abruptly to drag his hand over his face. "Tennis," he muttered. "That's all the woman thinks about."

Serena folded her arms over her chest, her short, square fingernails digging into her skin through the silk blouse. "It's my career," she said. "My life."

Alex hit his fist into his palm. "No! Your career, yes. But it should never be your life. That way you only end up half a woman, damn it. Can't you see that?"

"Half a woman?" Serena found control an endangered species as she repeated his words through clenched teeth. "Half a woman? Which half were you trying to lure into your bed only a short time ago?"

As her words reverberated around her head like an unwelcome echo in the small, cozy room, Serena sucked in several deep, calming breaths. What on earth was wrong with her? She never lost her temper. Never shouted. Serena Lawrence was the *Ice Princess*. Cool, composed, dignified. She would never, ever scream like a fishwife.

Alex was the first to regain some semblance of composure. "Are you quite finished?"

"Quite," she replied frostily. "And you?"

Despite his lingering frustration, Alex wanted to reach out and touch her, to love her, to smooth away the acrimony still hanging between them. He slipped his hands into his pockets. "For now."

She tilted her chin. "What does that mean?"

"It means, my sweet, that this is only the end of the first set. We'll continue the match sometime when you're more reasonable."

Temper flashed in her eyes, hot and unrestrained. When he smiled at her response, Serena realized she had been expertly baited.

"That's a good idea," she ground out. "A few hours' sleep will allow you time to regain your composure and enable us to continue this conversation like two intelligent adults."

As she turned to leave, Serena suddenly remembered that Alex was leaving for Washington in the morning. And in three days, she was scheduled to leave Claremont as well. The thought that she'd never see him again delivered a harsh, unexpected pain.

As she glanced back over her shoulder, Alex couldn't miss the distress lacing those lovely soft eyes. Shaking his head at the futility of this relationship, he spanned the slight distance between them. They stood toe to toe, each waiting the other out.

"Have a good conference."

"You'll knock 'em dead in Italy."

They laughed uneasily as they both spoke at once. Then Alex slowly brushed his knuckles along her cheekbone. "You're going to do fine," he assured her. "If your arm wasn't one hundred percent, you would have found it out today." His smile offered encouragement. "First Italy. Then the French. Then Wimbledon."

Serena returned his smile, lulled into a sense of safety by his gentle touch and tender words. Later she would tell herself that she should have known better than to drop her guard.

Alex drew her into his arms for a long, lingering kiss that Serena could no more have resisted than she could have flown to the moon.

"And then," he said into her ear, "it will be time to get on with our own match." This time his grin was fast and dangerous, reminding Serena of a wolf on the prowl. "You may be an undisputed winner on the tennis courts, Serena, my love. But you're going to discover that the game of life provides a few unexpected surprises."

The realization that Alex was promising not to disrupt her life until after she had the tour's toughest tournaments under her belt gave Serena the courage to take his words lightly.

She pressed her fingers against his smiling lips. "That may be," she said. "But I have a few trick shots you haven't seen. And of course you could always double fault."

With that she slipped out of the house, refusing to give in to an almost overwhelming urge to sneak a glance over her shoulder. If she had, Serena would have seen Alex watching her thoughtfully, a slight frown darkening his brow.

8

IT WAS RAINING in Washington, D.C. Not hard enough to flood all the streets, but enough to disrupt traffic. It took Alex an unreasonably long time to get from the dinner at the French embassy to the Georgetown home of Patrick and Carly Ryan. When Patrick had heard his friend was coming to town, he had insisted Alex cancel his reservations at the Shoreham and stay at the Ryan home. Alex had accepted the invitation gladly.

Using the key that Patrick had given him his first night in Washington, Alex heard the sounds of an argument in progress as he entered the house.

"Patrick Ryan, you louse, how can you take advantage of a woman in my condition?"

The aggravated feminine accusation was followed by a deep, low chuckle. "If I hadn't taken advantage of you, Carly, my sweet, you wouldn't *be* in that condition."

Alex grinned as he heard Carly's answering laughter over the driving beat of Miles Davis's jazz trumpet. Patrick and Carly might have been one of the most mismatched couples he had ever met, but their personalities complemented each other perfectly. Carly had brought sunlight and laughter back into Patrick's life after the tragic death of his first wife.

In turn, Patrick had contributed his vast store of inner strength to the marriage, providing an anchor Carly had been missing all her life. That they loved each other deeply was readily apparent. Alex had loved them both for years. The idea that they would be parents before the summer was over pleased him immensely.

Carly's sharp gaze caught Alex attempting to slip past the living room to the stairs. From the intimate tones of the conversation, he had assumed they would be wanting privacy.

"Alex, you're just in time," she proclaimed. "Come in here and tell Patrick that he's a cad to make me pay hotel rentals on Boardwalk."

"Patrick, you are a cad to make this luscious woman pay hotel rentals on Boardwalk," Alex answered obediently as he entered the room. They were seated on the floor, a Monopoly board between them. The green and red buildings dotting the board suggested that they had been playing for some time. The colorful stack of bills next to Patrick told its own story.

"So much for faithful friends," Patrick growled, shooting him a mock glare. "I thought I could at least count on you to back me up."

Alex grinned good-naturedly. "I never could resist Carly anything."

"Neither can I," Patrick admitted. He handed the dice to his wife. "Roll again."

She leaned across the board to kiss him. "That's very sweet of you, darling."

"Don't mention it. You'll get your opportunity to pay up later." His blue eyes filled with a lazy, sensual invitation.

"Mr. Ryan," Carly said with a laugh, "I do like your style."

Rolling the dice, she moved her top hat six spaces, landing on Go. As Patrick obediently counted out her two hundred dollars, she glanced up curiously at Alex.

"You're certainly home early. How was the dinner?"

Alex shrugged as he lounged in a gaily upholstered wingback chair. The once stiffly formal living room bore evidence of Carly's influence. The furniture was covered in bright prints, the walls were alive with blazing colors and he knew, were he to lift up the corner of the Oriental rug, he would discover scuff marks on the parquet floor from Carly's tap shoes.

"Excellent, as usual," he answered. "Although I've grown accustomed to California cuisine; all those sauces seemed a lot heavier than they used to."

"California seems to agree with you," Patrick said.

"It does," Alex replied. "To tell you the truth, I'm surprised to find that I'm actually enjoying the academic life. I was afraid I'd find it boring, but the students' enthusiasm is contagious."

Patrick nodded. "I told you so," he said to his wife.

Alex's curious gaze moved from Patrick to Carly and back again. "What's that supposed to mean?"

"Carly thought you seemed unhappy."

"I didn't say unhappy," Carly corrected. "The word was distracted." Her dark blue eyes studied Alex thoughtfully. "For instance, it's not like you to return so early from the French embassy. Didn't you used to date someone there? What was her name? The Brigitte Bardot look-alike."

Alex shot her a friendly scowl. "Monique. And I hadn't realized you kept such close track of my love life."

"It became ever so much easier once I got my personal computer," she countered blithely. "What's the matter, wasn't Monique invited to dinner?"

"She was there."

"But?" Carly encouraged.

Patrick put his hand on her shoulder. "Honey, Alex's personal life isn't any of our business."

She waved away his softly spoken protest. "Pooh. If he hadn't interfered and helped me convince you what a perfect wife I'd make, we might never have gotten married, Patrick Ryan. And just where would that leave Junior?" She patted her rounded stomach with undisguised feminine satisfaction.

"How is my godson?" Alex asked, sensing an opportunity to change the subject.

"Terrific," Patrick said proudly. "But how else could he be? You know Carly always adds her own special flair to whatever she does." He smiled at his wife, who grinned happily back.

"I'll bet the senator's tickled pink."

"He's already got his grandson's entire political career plotted. In fact, if my father has his way, the kid'll run for nursery-school president. At least having a new generation of Ryans to mold into politicians has taken the pressure off me." Patrick's lips curved in a wry grin. "Of course, I have to admit, I wouldn't mind being the father of the nation's chief executive."

His eyes brightened with a look Alex remembered seeing in Senator Mike Ryan's gaze every time he had attempted to force his son from the business world into the political arena. The two men had fought over the subject for years before the senator had finally accepted the idea that Patrick had the right to make his own life. Alex knew that, despite Patrick's words, this child would be encouraged to follow his own star.

"You and the senator are both going to be disappointed," Carly declared, grimacing as the baby moved under her hand. "This kid's going to be a field-goal kicker for the Redskins. He's been practicing steadily for the past two months."

Alex was fascinated by the movement under Carly's scarlet sweater. "May I?"

Her eyes were filled with affection. "Be my guest. It's about time he got acquainted with his godfather." As he joined her on the floor, Carly took Alex's hand and placed it on her abdomen.

"Michael Joseph Ryan," she said formally, "I'd like you to meet Alex Bedare, the nicest man in the entire world. With the exception of your daddy, of course," she corrected quickly as Patrick cleared his throat. With her words, the baby moved and Alex found himself deeply touched by the life stirring beneath his fingertips.

"He likes you," Carly said with a smile. "Which just proves what I've been saying all along. He's a very clever child."

When there was no sign of humor in her tone, Alex rocked back on his heels, eyeing her curiously. "You are kidding."

"She's not," Patrick stated. "Carly is convinced that children begin their learning process in the womb. She spent the first three months teaching him the alphabet. She's now worked her way up to reading him the sports page from the *Post* every morning."

"I just want him to realize how badly the Redskins need him," she said airily. "Besides, football games make far more interesting reading than the *Congressional Record*."

Patrick's gently teasing expression turned incredulous. "Don't tell me—"

Carly nodded. "While you were locked in that meeting with the labor council last night, the senator sat in that very chair and read aloud for two solid hours." She slanted a wry grin downward. "I didn't know how to tell your father, Patrick, but Junior fell asleep after the first ten minutes."

They shared a laugh before Carly demonstrated that, despite her rather fey personality, she could hone in on a problem with deadly accuracy.

"So," she said, eyeing Alex soberly, "what's bothering you?"

He glanced over at Patrick, seeking assistance. "I had almost forgotten how she never lets go of a topic."

"Like a bull terrier with a bone," he agreed. "You may as well open up, pal. None of us are going to be allowed to go to bed until you do."

Alex rose and began pacing the room. As Carly and Patrick exchanged a look, hers said *I told you so*, while his acknowledged her correct assessment of the situation. By unspoken agreement, both remained silent, giving Alex time to collect his thoughts.

The pulsating rhythm of Miles Davis gave way to the slow, mellow blues piano of Oscar Peterson, reminding Alex that Carly had been the one to introduce him to jazz the first night they met, so many years ago. Recognizing what they had as something special, Alex had never asked to be anything but Carly's friend and when she coincidentally fell in love with the man who had been his best friend for almost half his life, Alex had been the first to wish the couple the best of everything. During their tumultuous courtship they had both shared their problems with him. How could he fail to do likewise?

"It's a woman," he admitted finally.

"Anyone we know?" Patrick asked.

Alex stared out into the well of darkness. The rain continued to fall, slow and ceaseless, in rippling films of water that rolled down the window.

"I don't think so. You've probably heard of her, though. Her name's Serena Lawrence."

"The tennis player?" Carly asked.

"The one the press called the Ice Princess?" Patrick added.

"Right on both counts."

"Is she?" Carly inquired, unable to miss the frustration etching deep lines into Alex's brow.

She knew that Alex was not acquainted with rejection. If this Serena woman had refused his advances, it would undoubtedly irritate him. But Carly instinctively felt something else was going on here. He had been too quiet, too introspective since his arrival in Washington two days ago.

His gaze was still directed out the window, but only Alex knew that he was seeing Serena's face. That lovely, lovely face. "Is she what?"

Patrick grasped Carly's hand, squeezing her fingers. Characteristically she ignored the silent warning, believing that the only way to solve a problem was to face it straight on.

"Is she cold? Untouchable."

He spun around, his expression a mask of frustration. "No. Not really. She acts that way. Sometimes she almost has me believing that she's really as cool and composed as she behaves. But inside, deep down where it matters, she's a warm, passionate woman." He raked his fingers through his hair. "But I can't get her to put aside the barriers and allow any real intimacy."

"So you consider her a challenge," Carly pressed on.

"It started out that way," Alex admitted. "What man wouldn't like to be the one to unleash hidden fires in a beautiful woman?"

"What man indeed," murmured Patrick. His intimate gaze caused a warm flush to darken Carly's cheeks.

"But then she got under my skin, and all I know now is that the woman is driving me crazy." He shook his head with mute frustration.

Carly jumped to her feet, her movements graceful, despite the encumbrance of pregnancy. She flung her arms around Alex's neck, hugging him as close as possible, taking into account her jutting abdomen.

"You're in love!" she exclaimed. "I'm so very, very happy for you!"

Alex's hands went to her shoulders as he put her a few inches away from him. "That's ridiculous." His voice grated with alarm.

"It's not at all ridiculous," she returned sternly. "I always knew that when you finally fell for a woman, you'd go tumbling head over heels." She patted his cheek fondly. "Don't worry, Alex, it's not fatal. You only feel like you're going to die. Once we convince Serena what a catch you are, she'll be begging you to marry her."

"Marry?" His dark eyes shot to Patrick, who was watching the events with a resigned expression on his face. "Are pregnant women always subject to flights of fantasy, or is your wife the exception?"

"I don't know," Patrick drawled. "It sounds to me as if Carly may have hit on something here. After all, she has been accused of having second sight."

"By her grandfather," Alex reminded him firmly. "A vaudeville magician who earned his living by fooling the eye with sleights of hand. The man was not psychic. And neither is Carly," he insisted.

"Don't forget," Patrick argued, "she knew I was in love with her long before I figured it out."

Alex was not prepared to give in that easily. "That doesn't count. Any fool with half a brain could see you were crazy in love with her. Sorry, Carly," he said as he realized he'd just referred to her in a less than flattering light. "But your feelings were written all over your face in letters a foot tall, Patrick."

Patrick rose to his feet. "Try looking in the mirror, my friend," he said quietly. He put his arm around his wife's shoulder. "Ready to go upstairs?"

She smiled up at him. "That's an excellent idea. I've had a backache all day. You can rub it for me."

"I'd love to." His gaze promised far more than that and as they exchanged a loving glance, Alex was struck by an uncharacteristic surge of envy. Followed by what he reluctantly recognized as yearning.

Carly went up on her toes to kiss Alex. "Good night, dear. I know it hurts," she said gently. "But believe me, it will get better. You could never fall in love with a less than intelligent woman, Alex. Given time, she'll realize what a prize you are."

Alex had often considered that Carly Ryan, née Ashton, was the nicest person he had ever met. In all the years of their friendship, he had only been given additional reasons to maintain that belief. He managed an answering smile as he looked down into her earnest face.

"And if she doesn't?"

Carly dug into the pocket of her maternity jeans, pulling out a coin, which she placed into his palm, closing his fingers over it.

Alex was undeniably moved as he opened his hand. "Your lucky coin," he said, his voice threatening to crack under the emotional strain. "You've kept that for years."

Carly's smile was beatific as she looked up at her husband. "What do I need with a lucky coin? I have everything I could possibly ever want."

Her soft gaze returned to Alex. "Since you're my very best friend, outside of Patrick, of course, I'll overlook those unkind things you said about my grandfather. He promised me that there was magic in that penny when he gave it to me, Alex. And despite your admittedly understandable skepticism, you'll discover he was telling the truth."

With that she turned and left the room. Patrick stayed behind a moment. "She's right, you know. On all counts." With that said, he followed Carly, leaving Alex to stare at the Lincoln penny resting in his palm.

SERENA HAD ALWAYS ENJOYED playing at the Foro Italico in Rome. In other countries, tennis steadfastly remained a polite, proper game, although the Americans were admittedly changing that image more each year. In fact, the crowd at Forest Hills had begun to take on the enthusiastic behavior of baseball fans as they cheered, drank their beer and cracked peanuts.

But if there had been a prize given to the most vocal, the most effusive fans, that award each year would have to have been given to the people filling the stands of the Foro Italico. The Italians, refusing to be stifled by propriety, booed. They cheered. Serena had even known them to throw pillows. But when she walked out onto the court, three years after winning the Italian singles title, they outdid themselves. It took the ball boys twenty minutes to clear the flowers from the red clay.

Despite the fact that the Romans were obviously thrilled to have their *principessa* back again, Serena realized this tournament would present its own challenge. The superb clay courts, second only to the hard courts of the Stade Roland Garros in France, served to remind her that tennis was ultimately a game of reduction as one player must finally make the other surrender.

Clay grabbed the ball, taking a bite out of it, slowing it down to allow three or four more shots per rally than usual. A player must be fit; her strokes must play true. Serena knew that before the day was out, she would discover whether or not her insistence on returning to the game was based on a truthful analysis of her abilities or merely wishful thinking.

As a rule, Serena enjoyed playing on clay. She appreciated the way the surface allowed her to play artistically, experimenting with strumming and stroking the ball. Clay was made for the various slices and spins she was known for, strokes that could prove disastrous on grass.

Her opponent for the opening round was a Czech known for her strength and a second serve harder and faster than most players' first serves. But Serena had played Nadia Tiriac before and knew her to be mentally lazy. She could come up with the most unbelievable shots, then turn around and miss a lob. Serena knew that, if her arm held out for the additional strokes it would take to finish the match, she could win. The key was to take it slow and steady. And not allow her brain to realize that her knees were shaking.

She was grateful that Marty had been released from the hospital in time to join her in Rome. Despite the graffiti-covered cast on his leg, he had already proven invaluable, bringing along his notebooks full of player information: their patterns and strategies, as well as their past performances against her. Facing Tiriac across the net, her first real opponent in more than two years, Serena felt as ready as she ever would be.

From Tiriac's first serve, Serena knew she was back where she belonged. She hit a backhand return that ticked the tape and caused Tiriac to mishit into the net. Not a flashy shot, the return nevertheless had the Italians on their feet, shouting praises for their favorite. As if spurred on by their enthusiasm, Serena hit winner after winner, dropping shots and backhand drives, reeling off six straight games to take the set at love.

The second set did not come as easily; Tiriac broke Serena's serve then held her own for a 6-5 lead. Serena took the following game, only to turn around and find herself down 40-love with Tiriac serving at triple match point. The crowd cheered as Serena put away an overhead. Double match point. Tiriac lost her concentration and double faulted. Fifteen thousand people breathed a collective sigh of relief.

Single match point. Those watching Serena coil for the start of her topspin backhand would later agree that it was as pure a moment as the sport of tennis had to offer. The stunning shot seemed to deflate Tiriac's spirit, allowing Serena to continue the game and emerge the winner. Another shower of blossoms greeted her victory.

"You blew her away." Lindsay greeted Serena as she escaped the crowd of reporters and headed into the locker room.

"It was a good match. I was lucky, though. Nadia really had me going in that second set before she lost it."

"She's that way," Lindsay agreed. "If she ever learns to concentrate, we're all in trouble. Want to go to dinner after the doubles? Erik Lindstrom knows a terrific little place not too far from the hotel."

"I'd feel like a fifth wheel," Serena demurred. "Besides, I thought I'd just order room service."

Lindsay stared at her. "Your first night in Rome and you're staying in?" she asked incredulously. "Besides, Erik and I aren't going to be the only ones. The whole gang's going."

Serena knew exactly what gang Lindsay was referring to. That group of players who always managed to bring the same intensity of their play off the court as on. She had never quite understood how they could party all night then play championship tennis the next morning. But inexplicably, a select few of them managed to do exactly that. Serena had seen Lindsay win more than one tournament while nursing a raging hangover.

"Thanks anyway, but I think I'll make it an early night."

Lindsay shrugged. "Whatever turns you on." She grinned sheepishly. "Uh, if you're not going, do you think you could see your way clear to lend me some cash?"

Serena shook her head good-naturedly. It was expensive on tour. Despite the fact that many people assumed they had their expenses taken care of, like football players or other team athletes, tennis players paid their own way. While all the players Serena knew, herself included, could be accused of watching their dollars carefully, the Australians were notorious for being so tight they squeaked. "Short arms and deep pockets" was the expression often used. And Lindsay, Serena remembered, was infamous for being the cheapest of her countrymen.

Not only had Serena never seen her doubles partner buy a soda during a tournament, Lindsay always made a point of taking extra bottles back to the hotel from the players' lounge. She had never, to anyone's recollection, been seen purchasing tennis balls and was renowned for not only using the tournament telephone for long-distance calls, but consistently returning tournament cars with the gas tanks empty.

"Have a good time," Serena said with a smile, handing her friend several bills.

"You are an angel," Lindsay enthused as the money disappeared into a pocket. "See you at three."

"Three," Serena agreed as she gingerly applied ice to her arm. It was undeniably sore and the muscles were in a state of fatigue. She wished that she hadn't agreed to play doubles with Lindsay quite yet. But Serena was not the kind of person to go back on her word. If she was lucky, their opponents would hit all the balls to Lindsay this afternoon.

SEVERAL HOURS LATER, as she soaked in a hot bath, Serena had to admit her wish had been foolish. Of course she would receive the majority of the shots; after her forced inactivity, their opponents would naturally expect Serena to be the weaker player. But she had surprised them, rising to the occasion with a stoicism that even her father would have had to acknowledge.

When the phone rang, she hoped that it wasn't Lindsay, attempting one last time to coax her into joining the party. All she wanted to do was eat a light dinner then crawl into bed and watch a movie on television. Serena had always found it intriguing that late-night movies were invariably the same all over the world. It brought credence to the global-village theory of television. She had seen *Casablanca*, her favorite film of all time, in at least five languages, never the slightest bit disturbed by her inability to understand Italian or French or Swedish. She knew all the dialogue by heart.

"Hello," she answered the telephone on a cautious note.

"You sound tired."

At the familiar voice, Serena's fingers tightened on the receiver. "I am a little," she admitted.

"You shouldn't have taken on the doubles matches this first time out."

Serena could hear the disapproval in Alex's tone. Ignoring the fact that she had been telling herself that same thing only this afternoon, she coated her words in ice.

"I don't believe that's any of your concern."

He ignored her frosty tone. "Everything about you concerns me," he said easily. "From the tip of your silky, pale-gold hair right down to those cute little pink toenails. How's the arm?"

"Sore. But holding up."

"Congratulations on your win."

"Thank you. But how on earth did you know so soon? It was only a first round. I can't believe it made the news."

"I kept calling a friend on the night staff of the *Post* every few minutes," he said. "Finally, about four this morning, he promised to call me as soon as it came off the wire if I'd just leave him alone long enough to get some work done."

The fact that he had been thinking about her most of the night was enough to make Serena forget the dull ache in her elbow for the first time today. "Oh. I appreciate your concern," she said lamely.

"Have you eaten?"

"Not yet."

"Going out?" he asked casually, but Serena thought she detected a bit more interest than the question warranted.

"Lindsay wanted me to. She and Erik Lindstrom and some others were going to try a new restaurant."

"Erik Lindstrom. Blonde, right? Good-looking guy from Sweden who won Wimbledon last year."

"That's Erik."

"Are you going?"

"No. I thought I'd order something from room service and watch television for a while."

"That's a good idea."

Alex's relief was so blatantly apparent in his voice that Serena couldn't help but laugh. "I thought you wanted me to get out and enjoy life more."

His deep voice rumbled in her ear. "With me. Not with some oversexed tennis jock."

Serena's answering laughter was lighthearted, musical. "I can't believe you're actually jealous."

"Believe it," he said, suddenly serious. "I've spent the past two days kicking myself for not canceling classes and flying over there to be with you."

"I think your flowers were a better idea," Serena answered looking over at the vase of American Beauty roses. "Less distracting."

"Do you have any idea how much I'm tempted to get on the first plane out of L.A.?" His voice rolled over her like a sensuous blanket, enveloping her in its lush folds.

"I think I do," she admitted. "But really, Alex, I'd rather you didn't."

"I know. The tournament." Serena could hear his sigh over the long-distance wires. "I don't just want to make love to you, Serena, although I'll admit that's high on my list of priorities. But there're so many things we could do together. Trevi fountain. Picnics in the Villa Glori. Strolling the gardens atop Janiculum Hill. Ah, Serena, how I'd love to show you Rome!"

"I'd like that," she heard herself agreeing.

"Next year I'm going to be there with you."

"Next year," Serena echoed, knowing as she did so that she was allowing her fantasies to run away with her.

The same way she had been doing since arriving in Rome. As her taxi had careened down the Via del Corso, Serena had found herself seeing the colorful sights as if for the very first time. Again and again she had wished Alex had been there to share them with her.

Just as she had wished he could have witnessed her victory today. Perhaps, Serena considered, if Alex had seen her play, if he had watched her in top form, he would understand why she couldn't possibly give up the sport. Why all her energies had to go to the one thing in her life that had meaning. That idea brought her full circle to the fact that there was no room in her life for an affair, no matter how appealing.

Alex misunderstood her soft sigh. "You need to get some dinner and some sleep. Good luck tomorrow."

"Thanks. For everything," she added softly.

"Oh, I almost forgot. Donovan sends his love. And a rather odd message."

"Tell him I love him, too. What message?"

"He told me to remind you of your promise. Does that make any sense?"

Serena remembered the conversation she and Donovan had shared concerning her future. Or lack of one, in her brother's eyes. It would be the height of folly to tell Alex that Donovan wanted her to go out and find a man to father her children. She could just imagine his response. She murmured something that could have been an acceptance of Donovan's message or a denial, but was enough to keep Alex from dwelling on the matter. Hating to break the connection, she said goodbye and gently hung up the receiver.

SERENA WAS FLOATING on air. In fact, she imagined she could have flown home from Rome without the aid of an airplane. She had won her first tournament in nearly three years. After all the self-appointed pundits had declared her career dead. Serena's only regret was that Lindsay had suffered an attack of food poisoning that first night on the town. As a result, she and Serena had been forced to default on their second-round doubles match the following day. Serena would have liked to have returned home with both prizes.

Although she had kept her apartment across the street from the North Carolina clinic, the idea of returning there alone, with no one to share in her pleasure, was admittedly depressing. For two years she had insisted on living a solitary existence. Now Serena was willing to admit that a little human companionship could be a nice thing.

Seeming to have read her mind, Donovan had telephoned before she left Rome, suggesting she change her ticket to allow her to fly into L.A. She could stay with him the few weeks between the Foro Italico and the French Open. Serena had instantly accepted, ignoring the little voice in the back of her mind that suggested her eagerness had more to do with Donovan's next-door neighbor than with her brother himself.

"How's everything in Claremont?" she asked as Donovan maneuvered the M.G. through the airport traffic.

"Alex is fine."

Serena's cheeks burned at his casual response. Was she really that transparent? "I wasn't referring to Alex. I was asking about your work. How's Gloria?"

"My work's fine. Gloria, too, if you discount the fact that she's refusing to accept the courtship of a handsome male gorilla on loan from the Cornell primate center. She insists on watching that damn television."

"So take the control away."

Donovan swore softly and stepped on the brakes as a delivery truck cut in front of them. "I tried that only to discover that taking her off those cop shows cold turkey was the wrong thing to do. She was so furious that she gave poor Troilus a black eye the minute he tried to get the slightest bit amorous."

"Troilus?"

Donovan shrugged. "They're a literary bunch at Cornell." He glanced over at her as the sports car idled at a red light. "Since you weren't asking about Alex, you're probably not interested in knowing he's out of town again."

"Oh, really?" She forced a casual tone. "So where is your jet-set neighbor off to this time?"

"Mexico City. Something about the World Bank."

If she was distressed to find Alex filling her thoughts all too often while she was in Rome, Serena was appalled to discover how depressed she was to learn that he wasn't waiting in Claremont to welcome her home.

9

"OH, A LETTER ARRIVED for you today," Donovan said as they entered the house.

"From Mexico City?" Try as she might, Serena could not keep the hopeful note from her voice. She was grateful when Donovan failed to notice.

"Uh-uh," he answered absently, looking around the room. "It was from the White House."

"The White House?" Serena asked disbelievingly. "As in the Washington, D.C., White House?"

Donovan nodded as he dug through the papers scattered over the top of the ancient rolltop desk. "I know it's here somewhere," he muttered.

Serena grabbed his arm to get his attention. "Donovan, are you kidding me? Because, so help me, if you are—"

He gave her a wounded look. "I wouldn't kid about a thing like this, Serena."

"Then where is it?"

His gaze circled the room distractedly. Eyeing the clutter, Serena found it difficult to maintain hope that they would discover her letter in this lifetime.

"When did it arrive?" she asked, hoping to trigger some absent spark of memory. "What day?"

A triumphant light gleamed in her brother's green eyes. "This morning."

Now they were getting somewhere. "This morning. All right, what were you doing when it was delivered?"

Deep furrows gathered in Donovan's smooth brow. "I can't remember."

"Donovan Kincaid!" Serena's voice rose at least an oc
tave. "Think! What were you doing? This morning."

"I had breakfast with the apes," he said helpfully.

Serena groaned inwardly. If any of Donovan's beloved
charges had gotten hold of her letter, it was bound to be lost
forever.

"Did you have the letter then?" she asked, dreading the
answer.

"Of course not. The mail never arrives until after ten
o'clock, Serena."

She exhaled a deep sigh of relief. So far, so good. "All right,
then, what did you do after breakfast?"

"I talked with Gloria for a while."

"You mean talked *to* her," Serena corrected absently, her
mind still whirling with possible answers to who at the White
House could possibly be writing to her.

"With her," Donovan stressed. "Didn't I tell you? Gloria
has a working vocabulary of over twelve hundred words."

"Terrific. Maybe she can tell us where my letter is," Serena
muttered. "Come on, Donovan, this is serious!"

"So is my work with Gloria," he protested, clearly af
fronted.

"You're expecting me to believe that monkey—excuse me
ape—can talk?" Serena's disbelief was written all over her
face. She knew that Donovan could be considered eccentric
from time to time, but this was ridiculous.

"Not exactly talk," he admitted. "She uses a combination
of signs and computer symbols. We've just begun working
with the computer, but I've got high hopes for the results. She
really picks things up fast."

"Perhaps she picked up my letter."

"I told you that the mail came after I worked with her."

"That's right, you did," Serena said, feeling more and more
like Alice after she'd gone through the looking glass. Why was

Donovan looking at her as if she were the absentminded one? "So, what did you do after that?"

"I brought home the leftover fruit and made juice. I remember because there was an accident on the corner. A car hit a power pole and knocked out the electricity just as I was running the kiwi through the food processor."

"How did you know that's what happened?"

"Simple. I heard the collision and went out and looked down the street. It was a Porsche. A classic," he tacked on, his expression displaying remorse for the battered sports car. "A beauty, too. I felt real sorry for the driver."

Serena momentarily forgot her own concerns. "I hope he wasn't hurt?"

"No. But, Serena, you should have seen that car twisted around the pole. It was enough to make a grown man cry."

Knowing how Donovan felt about his ancient M.G., Serena could understand how her brother felt, but this conversation was not helping her find her missing letter.

"So, you went outside to look at the accident," she continued, picking up the scattered threads of the disjointed story. "What did you do next?"

She could almost see the wheels turning in his head. "Went back into the house. No, wait a minute," he said. "I picked up the mail and then I went into the house."

Bingo. She was definitely on the right track. "Then?"

He gave her a blank look. "I can't remember."

"Donovan!"

"Serena," he said amiably, "you know I can't think when you get hysterical."

Serena ground her teeth. "Donovan, dear," she said with saccharine sweetness, "please try to put yourself in my place. You've just returned from a long and wearying trip. You're suffering from exhaustion, not to mention jet lag. Your brother, whom you admittedly adore, despite his little eccentricities, tells you that somewhere around this place you've got a letter from the White House. Perhaps even the president. Of the United States," she added for emphasis. "How do you think you'd feel?"

"Thirsty," he answered promptly.

It was not the answer Serena had been expecting. "Thirsty?" she asked weakly.

"After I came back into the house, I realized I was thirsty. So I went into the kitchen for a glass of juice." Donovan's face split in a broad grin. "I think I know where the letter is." He held up a hand. "Wait right here."

Donovan was back in seconds, a square white envelope in his hand. When Serena took it from him, she lifted an eyebrow. The envelope was ice cold.

"It was in the freezer. Along with my gas bill," he admitted. "Good thing I found it before they turned my gas off, huh?"

"I have a hard time believing you'd even notice." Serena opened the frozen envelope and quickly scanned the letter inside. "Oh, my God, I can't believe it!"

"What's the matter?"

"Nothing's the matter. Donovan, I'm invited to dinner at the White House. With the president."

"Really?" Donovan's eyes brightened with enthusiasm.

"Really. Listen to this: 'The President and the First Lady request the pleasure of the company of Miss Serena Lawrence at dinner on Monday evening, April 27 at eight o'clock. Black tie.'"

Serena sank down onto the sofa, ignoring the textbooks scattered over the cushions. "I can't believe it," she said weakly. "Me. Serena Lawrence. Having dinner at the White House."

"With the president," Donovan added significantly. "Serena?"

She was staring at the gold-embossed presidential seal at the top of the engraved invitation. "Yes?"

"I've had a request for a federal grant into the government that's been gathering moss for months. You don't think—"

"Don't even suggest it," Serena cut in, giving him a stern look.

Donovan grinned good-naturedly. "It was worth a try."

WHEN ALEX CALLED Serena from Mexico City that afternoon, he was puzzled and more than a little frustrated when her voice was even cooler than usual. He couldn't help wondering if she was angry that he hadn't called her every day of the tournament. He had wanted to. On more than one occasion he had picked up the telephone, only to put it down again, afraid that he would do something to take her mind away from her game. Whatever way he moved—forward or backward—he seemed to run into that icy wall.

When he hung up after the unsatisfactory phone call, he paced the floor of his hotel room, asking himself why he continued trying to break through Serena's layers of reserve. Even as he failed to discern an answer, he picked up the telephone and placed a long-distance call to Washington, D.C.

"Patrick," he said as his friend answered, "I'm about to ask you for a big favor."

Ten minutes later, when Alex hung up, he was smiling.

THE EMBOSSED INVITATION had read eight o'clock. By seven, Serena was dressed and pacing the floor of her room at the Mayflower Hotel. She had spent the afternoon at a neighborhood beauty salon, where a bully named Mr. Hugo had labored for the better part of two hours with shampoo, conditioner, gel, mousse and spray, defying nature as he forced Serena's straight blond hair into a mass of curls atop her head, all the time assuring her that her usual casual style would never do. The fact that his clients routinely dined at the executive mansion appeared to make him an expert on White House appearances.

Serena, not a little intimidated by the dapper Frenchman, had enthusiastically professed her appreciation for his herculean efforts. Then she had returned to the hotel where she immediately drowned Mr. Hugo's frothy creation under the shower.

Now her smooth blond cap of hair curved under her chin as usual, her lids were dusted with a pale shade of blue shadow that she had purchased in the hotel gift shop for the occasion and her normally dark lashes had been treated to a coat of mascara. Anticipation had brought a rosy hue to her cheeks, making Serena decide to forego the wine-tinted blusher the shop clerk had insisted she buy. Clear gloss made her lips shine invitingly. She stopped her pacing long enough to look into the mirror.

"Cinderella's ready for the ball," she said aloud. Now all she had to do was to get through the next forty—correction, thirty-eight—minutes until her escort, a White House marine, arrived. A moment later there was a knock at the door.

"You're early," she said with a smile as she opened the door. Serena's mouth dropped open as she viewed Alex, resplendent in evening dress standing before her.

"Want me to go away and come back later?"

"What are you doing here?"

He handed her the gilt florist's box. "Do you always welcome your White House escorts with such enthusiasm?"

"You're supposed to be a marine," she said dumbly, still unsettled by his unexpected appearance.

"Sorry." He took the box back and turned to leave. "I didn't realize that your requirements were so stringent."

"Wait!" Serena's fingers curved around his arm. "Don't go I was just surprised to see you. Come in."

"If you insist." He entered the hotel room, stopping a few feet inside the door to study her more closely. "You look absolutely lovely."

She ran a hand down the skirt of her black crepe gown. The V neckline allowed an enticing but not abundant view of creamy skin and the long sleeves ended in points at her wrists, successfully hiding her scar. The dress was deceptively simple, cut on the bias to make the most of her feminine attributes.

"Thank you. Can you tell that I'm quaking in these high heels?"

His eyes moved down her body in a slow tour that did nothing to calm Serena's already taut nerves. "You're a vision of serenity," he assured her. "Sexy serenity," he corrected as he observed the way the soft material clung to her slender curves.

Serena's hand went to her throat. "Oh, dear, you don't think I've overdone it, do you? I've never been to anything like this."

He chuckled, pleased that Serena was allowing her human side to show through her facade of calm perfection. Perhaps he had only misinterpreted her cool tone the other day.

"The dress is perfect." His voice thickened. "The lady is perfect."

Serena's rippling sigh was easily heard in the sudden stillness of the room. "I missed you."

Alex felt as if Christmas had suddenly arrived eight months early. "Really?"

"Really."

He put the box down onto the cherry Queen Anne desk. "Enough to kiss me hello?"

Her eyes gave him the answer first as they deepened to a hue resembling polished pewter. "Oh, yes," she said, moving into his outstretched arms.

Heaven. His touch was nothing less than blissful, replenishing her spirit, filling a void that she had never known existed until she met him. She had expected Alex to crush her mouth quickly, hungrily. Instead, he surprised her by drawing her gently into his arms and pressing his lips against her hair.

"I've been miserable without you," he murmured.

She tilted her head back to look up at him. "I almost believe you mean that."

"Believe it." The turbulence swirling in his eyes as they locked onto hers was in direct contrast to his quiet voice. "I couldn't sleep for thinking of you, I couldn't work for wanting you. If you're trying to drive me crazy, Serena Lawrence, you're succeeding admirably."

Need. She could feel it in the strength of his fingers as they tightened on her waist. She could see it in the darkening storm of his eyes, hear it in the rough, gravelly sound of his voice. Serena had no trouble recognizing Alex's hunger because that same desire was thrumming through her body like a live wire, hot and dangerous.

"Show me." As she lifted her arms to comb her fingers through his thick black hair, the gesture fit her body more closely against his. "Show me how crazy I make you."

Lonely days and even lonelier nights contributed to a full-scale explosion as their lips met, consuming Serena in a blinding fire. Fantasies imagined but denied flashed before her mind's eye, erotic, vivid, demanding. She was alive—vibrantly, brilliantly alive—every nerve reaching for his touch, every pore seeking relief from a desire too long suppressed.

Primitive urges coursed through her as her hands fretted over him, thrusting under his jacket to pull his shirt free before roving heatedly over his back.

"Yes," she whispered, her avid mouth skimming over his face. "Yes, yes, yes."

A haze had settled over Serena's mind, a shimmering, hypnotizing golden cloud whose light was magnified by the feel of those strong hands cupping her curves, lifting her into the hardening strength of his body. There was no past, no present, only this glorious moment of anticipation. She had never wanted anything in her life like she wanted this man at this precise moment in time. That was why, when he suddenly released her, Serena felt as if she had just been dashed with a bucket of cold water.

Her hand fluttered at her throat as she tried to focus on the man who had left her to stand at the window, leaving her to stare at his rigid back as he looked down at the street.

Serena swallowed. "I don't understand."

She could see the rise and fall of his shoulders as he fought to control his breathing. When he turned to her, his expression was oddly devoid of emotion. If it hadn't been for the lingering turmoil in his dark eyes, Serena would have thought she had imagined the entire thing.

"I'm sorry. I didn't mean for that to happen."

She still didn't understand. "I wanted you to kiss me, Alex." She took a deep breath, determined to continue before she lost her nerve. "I wanted you to make love to me."

A muscle quivered in his jaw, but his unreadable expression did not change. "And now?"

"I still want you to make love to me." Unable to resist touching him, Serena crossed the room to frame his face in her palms. "I spent the entire time in Rome wanting you," she said quietly. "I lay awake nights thinking of nothing else. I didn't want to feel this way. It frightened me. It still does."

She managed a soft smile that Alex realized was directed inward. "You were right, Alex. I've been fighting my feelings for you since the night we first met. But I can't any longer. I want to make love with you. Here. Now."

Alex had remained silent, not wanting to interrupt Serena's stunning admission. Before he could come up with an appropriate response, police sirens accompanying a motorcade through the streets below recaptured his unwilling attention.

"And what shall we tell the president?" he asked, forcing a light tone.

Color rose in Serena's cheeks as she dropped her hands and ran to the nearest mirror. "The president! Oh, my God, how could I have ever forgotten about him?" She picked up a brush and began moving it wildly over her hair.

Alex came up behind her. "Perhaps you had other things on your mind."

Her eyes met his in the mirror. "Perhaps that was it," she agreed.

Warm ebony eyes caressed soft, silvery gray in the glass. "There's always later," he suggested.

Serena lowered the brush and turned toward him. Going up on her toes, she brushed her lips against his. "Later."

"I must be losing my touch," he grumbled as he went to retrieve the florist's box from the desk. "My timing definitely leaves a lot to be desired lately."

"Speaking of timing, what are you doing here?" she asked. "I didn't expect to see you again."

"I warned you that you weren't going to get rid of me that easily," he said with a smile as he fastened the single orchid around her wrist.

"Still, Alex," Serena protested, "how did you manage to cancel my marine and take his place?" She paled as an unwelcome idea suddenly occurred to her. "You didn't wait downstairs and offer him a bribe or anything, did you?"

"Of course not."

"And you didn't have him kidnapped?"

His only answer was a look of pure censure.

"You're right," Serena admitted. "That would be excessive behavior, even for you."

"Thanks. I think," he muttered.

At least things were back to normal. Alex hadn't thought he would be able to sit through the long, boring evening feeling as he had only a few minutes ago. He supposed he ought

to be grateful to Serena for bringing them back to earth, but
a part of his mind wished that she wasn't so adept at turning
off her feelings.

"So how did you do it?" She began to put on a pair of pearl
earrings.

"I've still got a few connections. Wait a minute." Alex took
the pearl from her hand.

Serena cast a frustrated glance down at the slender gold
watch circling her wrist. "I don't want to be late, Alex."

He decided that for the sake of peace he would not point
out she had forgotten entirely about the White House dinner
earlier. "I have something for you," he said instead. He
reached into an inside jacket pocket and took out a small
black box.

"Oh, Alex," Serena breathed reverently, gazing down at
the twin diamond studs blinking back from a bed of ebony
velvet. "They're beautiful." She closed the lid decisively. "But
much too expensive. I can't accept."

"Of course you can," he argued, reopening the jewelry box.
"I was shopping for a welcome-home present for you when
these caught my eye. They're you, Serena."

Ignoring her soft sound of protest, Alex slipped them into
her earlobes. Putting his hands on her shoulders, he turned
her back toward the mirror. "How coolly they glitter," he
murmured, brushing her hair back from her face. "Like chips
of ice. But when you move your head even the slightest bit,
they capture the light and turn it into fire."

She was unable to resist staring at the shards of light
emanating from the perfectly cut stones. "They're just like
you, Serena Lawrence," Alex said quietly. "Cool ice and
brilliant flame. If you don't accept them, I'll simply have to
throw them away. They'd never suit another woman as well
as they do you."

Serena gasped at that. "You wouldn't really?" she protested, her fingers moving to her ears unconsciously, as if to protect the lovely diamonds from his rash actions.

"Of course I would."

She shook her head. "The crazy thing about all this is that I almost believe you."

"Then you'll keep them?"

"Do I have any choice?"

The familiar laughing light was dancing in his eyes. "No."

Serena crossed the room to the closet, pulling her wrap from the hanger. "So what else is new?"

Alex grinned unrepentantly. "I knew you'd see things my way."

As they left the room, Serena had to admit that his arrogance was well-deserved. She capitulated so easily where he was concerned. While she didn't like the atypical behavior Alex stimulated, she had to admit that, at the present time, she was helpless to change things. She vowed that beginning tomorrow morning, she would take the steps necessary to bring their relationship onto a more even footing. But for tonight, this one magic night, she was going to reach out with both hands for whatever life had to offer.

10

MAGIC. SERENA COULDN'T REMEMBER ever experiencing a night so memorable. The events were bathed in a warm glow, as if she were viewing them through a rose-tinted haze. Seated at the first lady's table along with the president of France, Serena also had an opportunity to chat with the president and was given a tour of the White House rose garden. She danced with the vice president, the secretary of state, and Julio Iglesias. How many women had ever been so lucky, Serena thought to herself as the singer escorted her back to her table. She felt precisely like Cinderella before her gilt coach had turned back into a pumpkin.

"Can you believe it?" she said to Alex in the back seat of the limousine returning them to the Mayflower. "I, Serena Lawrence, danced with the vice president. Me." Her smooth brow furrowed. "Do you think he could tell that I was terrified of stepping on his toes?"

Observing the flush of excitement blooming in her cheeks, Alex decided he had never seen her look lovelier. "You looked like Ginger Rogers to his Fred Astaire," he assured her.

Serena gave him a quick, impulsive kiss on the cheek. "What a nice thing to say. Did you hear the French president invite me to visit him when I'm in Paris next month?"

"I did. I also heard you agree to take him up on the invitation. I hope you're not going to back out at the last minute."

Serena knew Alex was referring to her habit of tuning everything out but her matches while on tour. A secret part of her admitted that was probably what she would do. But she didn't want to think about that. Not now.

"Let's not argue tonight," she pleaded softly, placing her hand on his arm. "It's been so perfect; I don't want anything to spoil it."

He covered her hand with his, unable to resist her anything. "Agreed."

"What did you think of Julio Iglesias?"

"I thought he was holding you too damn tight."

Not for the first time, Serena experienced a surge of feminine satisfaction at the unmistakable jealousy in his tone. "I meant his voice. Don't you think he sounds even better in person?"

"It's hard to say." Alex shrugged uncaringly. "I never cared for him much myself."

Serena's gray eyes widened. "You're kidding! The man has a remarkable voice. Did you see the first lady? She actually had tears in her eyes when he sang 'Besame Mucho.'"

"It was probably just the Bermuda onions in the salad."

"You're just jealous." Serena softened her accusation with a smile. "You could have heard a pin drop in that room when he was performing. Everyone was entranced."

"Yeah, but can he play the ukulele?"

"What does that have to do with anything?" Serena asked blankly. "Oh, I see. I suppose this is your way of professing your own musical talents."

"I've been known to send a shiver down a feminine spine or two," Alex admitted offhandedly.

"With a ukulele?" she asked with blatant disbelief.

"With a ukulele," Alex repeated, his firm tone revealing that he would brook no further argument on the subject. "How do you think I managed to distract Gloria in order for your brother to steal the remote control the night of your charity match?"

The idea of Alex serenading Donovan's three-hundred-pound gorilla with a ukulele sent Serena into gales of silvery laughter. She was still laughing as the limousine pulled up in front of the hotel. Her smothered giggles drew a few interested glances as the elevator took them to the fifth floor, but by the time they entered her room she had managed to stifle all but her lingering smile.

"I'm glad to know I'm such a source of amusement," Alex said with mock severity, leaning back against the closed door.

At his injured frown, Serena's giggles broke forth again. "Oh, darling," she gasped, as she flung her arms around his neck, "you are so adorable when you make yourself all stiff and proper."

He wrapped his arms around her waist, trying to keep the smile from breaking loose as he gazed down into her breathtakingly lovely face. During the ride back to the hotel, Serena had made the stunning metamorphosis from an attractive, sedate young woman to a sexy, enticing siren. Alex had never seen anything quite so alluring.

"Stiff?"

"Like some Middle Eastern potentate," she alleged with a firm nod. "I feel as if I'm about to be banished from the harem for daring to laugh at my lord and master." Serena deftly untied Alex's black tie.

"It's a serious crime," he assured her soberly. "I've known certain sheikhs who'd beat a wife who had the effrontery even to smile at them the wrong way."

"That's barbaric," she protested. Her fingers disposed with the ebony studs gracing the front of his pleated dress shirt.

"Not barbaric, just the custom." Alex drew in a deep breath as she touched his skin. "Is this a private game, or can anyone play?"

Her eyes gleamed. "Two can play," she said, her voice half honey, half smoke. "Feel free to jump in whenever you're ready," she invited as she pushed the shirt off his shoulders, giving her a glimpse of his chest.

Alex pulled her against him, allowing her to feel the tumescent strength of his body. "I've been ready for weeks," he murmured. "Do you have any idea how difficult it's been for me to remain patient, to stay away, while I gave you time to make up your mind about us?"

She tilted her head back to look up at him, her expression suddenly serious. "It hasn't been easy on me, either."

Alex's dark eyes swept over her uplifted face in a slow, thoughtful perusal, which gave Serena the impression that he was choosing his next words very carefully. Then he shook his head.

"Alex?"

As he seemed to hesitate, Serena prayed silently, desperately, that Alex hadn't changed his mind. Not now. Not after she had bared her soul to him. Well, not exactly her soul, she admitted reluctantly. But it certainly hadn't been easy to reveal how much she had missed him. How she, too, had been waiting for this moment.

Alex's soft sigh was a gentle breeze against Serena's lips as he kissed her with tantalizing tenderness. Gone was his earlier passion. In its place was something new, something indefinable. Through the golden glow infusing her body, Serena attempted to put a name to the feeling as he ran the tip of his tongue around her parted lips. As it slid deftly between her teeth, sweeping the warm, moist vault of her mouth, conscious thought disintegrated and Serena surrendered to the rising heat created by his hands as they roamed her body with increasing intimacy.

Through the dazed senses she heard the whisper of metal as Alex lowered the zipper on her dress. A moment later it was a black-crepe pool around her feet. Before she could step out of it, Alex had lifted her into his arms and was carrying her to the king-size bed dominating the room.

Serena felt uncomfortably submissive as she lay on her back, exposed to his gaze. When she moved to cover herself with the sheet, Alex caught the edge, forestalling her action.

"Cold?"

"A little," she fibbed, unwilling to admit to the heat building in her.

He covered her breast with his palm in a vaguely possessive gesture. "You won't need the cover," he promised, his voice unusually rough. "I'll have you warm soon enough, love. With my hands." They caressed her slowly, tenderly, from her shoulders to her thighs. Without being aware of him removing it, Serena realized she was no longer wearing her bra.

"With my lips." He feathered teasing, tantalizing kisses over her face, causing the blood to glow under her skin. When his lips trailed slowly down her throat, his mustache teasing her flesh, a pinpoint flush of scarlet blossomed on her breasts.

As he took her rosy nipple between his teeth, Serena experienced an answering tug between her thighs. He hadn't lied about his ability to warm her. She was on fire; tongues of flame licked at her skin. Mindless of her need to appear controlled, composed at all costs, Serena tossed her blond head on the pillow as she lifted her hips from the mattress in mute appeal.

Alex's usual finesse disintegrated as he stripped her slip and panty hose from her with strangely trembling hands. His own clothing he managed to dispense of clumsily before returning to lie beside her on the mattress.

His mind scorched with need, Alex fought the urge to take Serena quickly. He had waited too long to rush this now. He wanted it to be the perfect conclusion to a perfect evening. Something that she would remember for the rest of her life.

"I've wanted you longer than I've ever wanted any other woman," he said as he brushed his lips against her throat.

"I've waited for you longer than I've ever waited for any other woman."

"I've wanted you, too," she whispered breathlessly.

"Oh, sweetheart, that's what I wanted to hear." His kiss was deep, drugging, triumphant. "So soft," he murmured after he had released her tingling lips. His palm grazed over the satin of her skin. "So very soft."

It was as if, once he had tasted of Serena's sweetness, Alex couldn't get enough of her. His mouth claimed hers again and again to drink longingly, thirstily. Serena's soft moan as his hand roved across her rib cage was swallowed in the depths of the increasingly passionate kisses.

"But you're strong, as well," he said thickly as he pressed his palm against her stomach. "It's a heady combination, Serena. There are those times, when you drop the Ice Princess facade, that you remind me of a soft, warm kitten. Wide-eyed and vulnerable."

A jolt of fear zigzagged through her. "No," she whispered, closing her eyes to his touch. Vulnerable was something she could never allow herself to be.

"Look at me, Serena." His fingers tangled in her hair as he held her wondering gaze to his. "You can allow yourself to be soft with me, honey. I'll never hurt you."

"You want my surrender," she managed to argue between parched lips.

"I want your *willing* surrender," he corrected gently. "As you'll have mine. I want more than just your body, Serena. I want everything you have to give. Not just your softness, but your strength as well. I love it when the purring little kitten turns into a tigress in my arms."

"I don't understand," Serena said helplessly as he rubbed the burgeoning tip of her nipple with the pad of his thumb.

"Neither did I, in the beginning." The fingers of his other hand trailed down to the juncture of her thighs. "I'll explain it to you later."

"But—"

"No more words." As he pressed his palm against the molten heat of her, Serena cried out softly. "Let me show you how I feel about you."

With a gentleness that belied his almost savage hunger, Alex coaxed her satiny thighs apart with his palms, settling himself between them. He entered her slowly, to savor every exquisite moment of their joining, stopping the instant he heard her gasp. His eyes gleamed with a fierce sensuality that would have frightened Serena had it not been for the tenderness of his tone.

"Just relax, love," he soothed, his hands stroking the taut muscles of her thighs. "Let me show you how good it can be." He slid one hand under her derriere, lifting her hips against him, allowing her time to adjust to his alien presence.

"Oh, Alex," Serena whispered, overcome by a spiraling vertigo she had never before experienced. "I can't."

"Yes, you can," he insisted as he began to move in a slow steady rhythm. "Trust me, Serena."

Alex experienced a surge of primitive satisfaction as he felt Serena's stiffness melting away under his increasingly driving force. Her fingernails dug into his shoulder as her legs wrapped around his hips. Her flesh was warm and moist against his, her breath a heated breeze as he kissed her again and again, his thrusting tongue echoing the movements of his body.

A pressure was building deep inside Serena, stretching her body tighter than ever before. She felt as if she were a smoldering volcano on the very brink of eruption.

"Alex, I can't stand any more. Please. It's too much."

He could feel the tenseness in her body; he could hear the desperation in her ragged voice. Every moan, every low cry, every unconscious movement she made as she tossed and writhed underneath him demonstrated that Serena was very near the brink. For that he was admittedly grateful. He wasn't certain how much longer he could hold back himself.

"You're almost there, love," he assured her, his strong hands grasping the soft skin of her hips and increasing his rhythm as he surged even deeper into her welcoming flesh. "Almost there. Just a little bit longer..."

"Ah," he breathed in satisfaction as he felt the rippling convulsions rip through Serena's body.

"Alex? Alex!" She clung to him fiercely, mindlessly giving herself up to the shimmering release.

Alex could not have imagined the pleasure to be found in Serena's passionate response to his lovemaking. He had finally breached the barriers she had erected between them, conquering her icy reserve even as he staked his claim on her for all time. She was his, his feverish mind cried out. All his.

A blood-red haze appeared before Alex's eyes as he followed her to his own tumultuous release, burying his lips in the soft hollow of her shoulder as he triumphantly called out her name.

SERENA WOKE TO FIND HERSELF alone in the wide bed. She sat up, her eyes circling the room, seeking Alex out in the pale pink light of early dawn. She found him seated in a chair across the room, a hotel towel wrapped about his hips. Until she heard her own sigh of relief, Serena had not realized how much she cared. How painful it would have been had he not been there.

Alex looked up as he heard the rustle of sheets. "Good morning," he said, trying out his voice, pleased to find it strong and steady.

Watching Serena sleep, Alex had suffered severe misgivings. He had not known what to expect from her this morning. During the long, love-filled night, she had come to him again and again, holding nothing back. But in the revealing light of day he had half expected Serena to scurry back behind her mental barricades.

She stretched luxuriously, reminding Alex of a sleek, lithe cat. "Good morning."

When Serena rose naked from the bed and came toward him, Alex felt a renewed stir of desire and wondered how he could still want her. Again and so soon. After all they had shared.

He rubbed Carly's coin between his fingers. He had found the lucky penny on the floor this morning. It had obviously fallen out of his pocket during their frantic undressing the previous night. When Carly had first given him the talisman, Alex had been moved by her generosity, but he had not believed in its alleged powers. This morning he was forced to wonder.

With a display of openness he would have found incredible only a day ago, Serena settled herself onto his lap and twined her arms around his neck.

"Are you as hungry as I am?" she asked.

"Hungrier."

Alex nibbled on her neck, breathing in the warm fragrance that was hers and hers alone. He had been attempting since that first night in the garden to pinpoint that scent. Last night it had come to him. Serena always smelled like a newly mown meadow after a gentle summer storm. Even now he could taste the rain on her skin.

He lowered his mouth to her breast and was rewarded as her pulse leaped in response. "Starving." She drew in a quickened breath as he took the rosy peak between his lips. "Mmm. Famished."

As Alex's tongue flicked over her flesh, dark, driving waves of need flooded over Serena. "I was speaking about breakfast," she protested raggedly, even as her hands were tangling in hair still damp from the shower, urging him on.

"Later."

His clever hands moved over her body, creating exquisite pleasures just this side of pain. Serena gave of herself willingly, without embarrassment or shame. She invited intimacies allowed to no previous man even as she demanded more. Gone was the controlled Ice Princess of the tennis world; in her place was a woman confident in her sensuality, passionate in her response. As Serena put away her past, so did she turn away from thoughts of the future. There was only now. Only this single, glorious moment.

Her own hands were not idle, skimming over him, tugging away the towel, reveling in the maleness of his body. Where she was soft, he was hard; where she had swelling curves, he was all lean muscle. Where her thighs were smooth, polished, his were hair-roughened, corded with taut sinews. Their desire made them the same, even as their bodies made them different. Male and female. Serena's woman to Alex's man. Each possessing a savage power that drove the other to the brink of madness time and time again.

Serena's head was spinning, her breathing fast and shallow. No longer did she know or care whether the gasps and sighs filling the air came from her own ravished lips or from his. She only knew that she was being drawn deeper and deeper into a swirling sea of sensations.

Alex's fingers dug into her hips as he shifted her on top of him. When he completed their joining with a mighty thrust, Serena thought her lungs would burst. As she felt herself drowning, she thought no more.

"I MADE THE PAPER!" Serena handed the page of the *Washington Post* to Alex. "Look, here's a picture of me dancing with the vice president."

Alex looked up from buttering his roll. "So it is," he agreed casually. "Want some more hot water for your tea?"

She reached out, plucking the roll from his hand. "What I want is for you to act a little excited."

He selected a blueberry muffin from the linen-lined basket to replace the roll she'd taken. "I'd love to oblige, sweetheart, but after the workout you've given me in the past ten hours, I need to recoup my strength." Dancing devils gleamed in his dark eyes. "The spirit's willing, but the body's pooped."

Alex was more than a little stunned when Serena stuck her tongue out at him. "Wretch. I don't know why I should have expected you to congratulate me on my White House debut. After all, for you it's old hat."

Serena picked up the paper again. She almost didn't recognize the sophisticated woman in the vice president's arms. "You could at least tell me that it's a decent photo. *I* think I look pretty good."

"You are the most beautiful lady the East Room has ever seen. In fact, you've probably brought the country to the brink of chaos. Government will grind to a halt as men leave their offices in droves to go knocking on doors all over town to search for you. Like hundreds of Prince Charmings seeking out Cinderella." He grinned. "Is that better?"

"Much better." She bit into a flaky croissant. "By the way, you never did tell me what you did to my marine escort last night. I half expected to find him out in the hallway this morning, tied and gagged."

Alex shrugged. "I called a friend of mine. He was able to pull a few strings."

Serena gathered the scattered crumbs from the croissant into the palm of her hand. "Is he in politics?"

"No. But his father is."

"I see," Serena said, not really seeing at all. She brushed the crumbs onto her plate before taking a sip of the peppermint tea. "Does this politician have a name?"

"Mike Ryan."

Serena's eyes widened and she lowered her cup to the bone-china saucer. "Alex, you know Mike Ryan?" A twenty-six-year veteran of the House of Representatives, Mike Ryan was as much a fixture around Washington as the Lincoln Memorial and the Smithsonian. The newspapers as well as the *Congressional Record* were peppered with his colorful quotes.

"His son Patrick is my best friend. Patrick's wife, Carly, comes in a close second." He put his napkin down on the table and leaned back in his chair, smiling broadly. "I'm going to be godfather to their first child in a few months."

It would have been impossible for Serena to miss the mixture of pride and joy that brightened Alex's features when he spoke of the Ryans' upcoming child. "You say first child as if there's already a plan to have more."

He flashed her a quick grin. "The subject is still open for discussion, although last time I heard, Patrick was hoping to field his own basketball team."

"That's a pretty big family, these days. Does his wife work?"

"Carly's a vice president of Capitol Airlines. She handles customer relations, press releases, things like that."

"Oh." Serena spread some butter atop an apple Danish. "I suppose they can hire all the help they need, then."

Alex thought he detected something in Serena's smooth tone, but he couldn't quite put his finger on what it was. Whatever, a small cloud was suddenly hovering over the table, threatening to darken the day that was dawning bright and sunny outside the window.

"I suppose so," he agreed easily. "Although if I know Carly, she isn't going to hand over the care of her child to a paid employee. She's already reading to him."

"Really?" She gathered the napkin from her lap and placed it on the table.

Slowly, inch by treacherous inch, he could feel the ice beginning to flow. What the hell was wrong with her now?

"Really. She's convinced children begin learning in the womb. What's the matter?"

"Matter?" The smile Serena gave him was guileless. And entirely false. "Why, nothing's the matter, Alex. Whatever do you mean?" She lifted her cup to her lips.

Alex wondered if Serena realized her voice took on a vaguely British accent whenever she began her transformation into the Ice Princess. He had never met Serena's father, but he'd bet his last cent that he knew the man's voice. Because at this moment it was coming out of Serena's lovely lips.

"You just seem a little disturbed," he offered.

Her hands trembled ever so slightly as she lowered the cup once again to its matching saucer. As the slight clatter gave her away, Serena knew better than to attempt to lie. It would be impossible with those intense black eyes locked onto her face.

"It's probably just all this talk about children," she said with a shaky laugh.

"Don't you like kids?" he asked with interest.

"Of course I do. Other people's," she clarified. When he looked puzzled, Serena felt the need to explain. "There's no room in my life for children. In the first place, it's a little difficult to play championship tennis when you're bounding around the court like an oversize water buffalo."

"Granted. But it's only a few months. Other women have taken time off to have children and returned to the tour, haven't they?"

"Yes, they have," Serena said impatiently. "But it's more than that. Children need so much love and care. It's a constant, never-ending task. And for a woman to attempt it alone—" Serena's voice dropped off.

An alarm suddenly sounded inside Alex's head. Of course, she was worried about getting pregnant. Why hadn't he thought of that? Because, Alex admitted, her response last night had caught him entirely off guard. He had come to the hotel, fully prepared to face an argument when she discovered that he was her escort. Not only had she willingly accepted that change in plans, but she had practically seduced him once they'd returned to the hotel.

All right. That explained his breach of caution last night. But what about this morning? After all they had shared, he couldn't very well claim ignorance. And he was definitely old enough, not to mention experienced enough, to have considered the matter of birth control. As Alex ran the question over and over again in his mind, he realized that the idea of Serena being pregnant with his child was undeniably appealing. If nothing else, he considered, knowing it to be a selfish thought, an unexpected pregnancy would create some very strong ties. If she was carrying his child, Serena would have no choice but to agree to spend the rest of her life with him. How long would it take before she knew, he wondered. Three weeks? Four?

He reached across the table and took her hand. "If anything happens, you wouldn't be alone, Serena." The idea of Serena's pregnancy took root, becoming more appealing with each passing moment.

The conversation had suddenly grown too personal. Serena slipped her hand from Alex's reassuring one and rose from the table. She went over to the window and gazed unseeingly down onto the street below where morning traffic jammed Connecticut Avenue.

"I never asked how long you're staying in Washington. Do you have a plane to catch this morning?"

Alex was watching her carefully. "I'm free."

"When do you have to get back to Claremont?"

"I'm well covered. It's finals week."

Lost in the turmoil of her own thoughts, Serena barely heard Alex's answer. "Oh."

A cab driver leaned on his horn as a pedestrian jaywalked, racing toward the escalators that led to the Metro, Washington's sleek, art-deco subway. To the casual onlooker, it would appear to be a normal day. People were hurrying to their offices, taxi drivers were defying any and all statutes of Washington's traffic code, a pair of pigeons perched on the windowsill, hoping for a few crumbs from a soft-hearted guest's breakfast. Nothing out of the ordinary. So why did Serena feel as if her life had been inexorably altered?

His words belatedly sunk in. "Don't you have to be there for the exams?"

"I wrote the exam two weeks ago. When I heard about your trip to Washington, I arranged to have a proctor sit in for me."

She turned around to eye him curiously. "Why on earth would you do that? Surely you've eaten dinner at the White House before."

"I wanted to be with you," he said simply.

"That's all?"

Alex smiled at her astonished disbelief. "I can't think of a better reason. Now, what do you want to do today?"

"Do?"

Extemporaneous behavior had never been Serena's forte. It had not been William Lawrence's manner of living, and Serena was, in nearly every respect, her father's daughter. She had always known precisely where she was going, what she was going to do with her life. She had never wavered off the path that had been carefully chosen for her. As a result, there had been few surprises. The accident, to be sure, was not part of the plan. But even then, Serena had gotten strength from the idea that she knew precisely what she was working toward. Her goals were still there, the course intact.

Yet since meeting Alex, more and more detours had appeared along the way to confuse her. She couldn't shake the feeling that last night she had stepped off the safe and narrow path entirely, opting for one that ran off in a new direction. Unknown. Little traveled. And certainly never by her. Uneasy was too mild a term to describe what Serena was feeling. Her eyes revealed her discomfort as she sorted through her answer.

"Serena?" Alex asked quietly. "It's up to you, honey. Anywhere you want to go." He grinned. "I've got my American Express card; the sky's the limit."

"Anywhere?" Serena asked hesitantly. Several possibilities came to mind. The Smithsonian, the National Gallery, Arlington. All standard tourist fare.

Alex could see a miniscule fissure opening in the wall Serena had tried to build between them only minutes ago. Telling himself that he should be grateful for small favors, he struggled not to push her in a direction she wasn't yet prepared to take.

"Anywhere," he repeated with a coaxing smile.

Her smile brightened the room like the sun coming out from behind the clouds after a long, dreary winter. *Why not*, Serena asked herself. This wasn't real, anyway. It was only a dream. A magical, glorious dream. And in dreams you could do whatever you wanted.

"The zoo."

A dark brow climbed his forehead. "The zoo?"

Serena nodded, crossing her arms over her chest as she leaned back against the windowsill. "The zoo," she repeated more firmly. "What's the matter, do you have something against animals?"

Alex laughed as he rose from the table and planted a long, lingering kiss against her lips. "How can you say that to a man who sings 'Abba Dabba Honeymoon' to a high mountain gorilla?"

Serena breathed a sigh of exquisite pleasure as she leaned her forehead against his shoulder. "How indeed?" she asked happily.

"I STILL FIND IT DIFFICULT to believe that you've never been to a zoo." Alex's voice mirrored his blatant disbelief that anyone could have suffered such a deprived childhood.

"Zoos are for weekends; I was always practicing on Saturdays and Sundays," Serena murmured, leaning over the railing to get a closer look at the panther pacing back and forth inside his compound.

"You realize that proves my point."

She glanced over at him. "What point?"

"That you've never had a life outside of that damn game."

Serena tossed her head in an angry gesture, knowing that he was baiting her and hating herself for responding. "No one ever held a gun to my head," she said stiffly, turning away to watch the panther once more. So much potential power, she considered, eyeing the narrow moat with a very real trepidation that for the moment made her forget that she was furious at Alex.

"Are you certain he can't jump that?"

Feeling the slight thaw, Alex put a reassuring arm around her waist. "Fairly sure. But don't worry, if anything happens, I'll protect you from him."

"Sure," she shot back. "But who's going to protect me from you?"

That earned a laugh. They fell silent, watching the lean black cat settle down in the sun atop a rock. Despite his lazy sprawl, energy radiated from his sleek ebony body. She could almost see it. Taste it. Serena knew that the jungle cat's relaxed appearance was deceiving; he was prepared to spring into action at the slightest provocation. It was thrilling to be only a few feet away from so much potential danger.

"You know, he reminds me a little of you," she murmured.

Alex flashed a grin. "I think I like that."

"You can take that smug look off your face. It wasn't all that complimentary a comparison. I was referring to his propensity to pounce."

"I never pounce," Alex objected.

"Never?"

"Never."

"I should have remembered you used to lie for a living."

"Lie?" He flung his hand against his chest. "You've wounded me, Serena. Deeply."

"I doubt that's possible," she countered dryly. "Besides, isn't that all a diplomat really is? A person who lies for his country?" Her brow furrowed in thought. "Who was it who said that a diplomat's job is to do the nastiest thing in the nicest way?"

"Isaac Goldberg," he answered. "I think this is where I tell you that I've never been particularly fond of that description."

"If the shoe fits," Serena returned mildly.

"I think I hate the way this conversation is going," he grumbled. "I thought you'd compared me to our sleek jungle friend to boost my ego."

Serena couldn't resist laughing at his downcast expression. "You, of all people, certainly don't need anyone to boost your ego."

"We could all use a little ego boost from time to time," he argued, taking her hands in his and drawing her to him. "Right now mine is lying in tatters down at the bottom of that moat. Didn't your mother ever teach you about the delicacy of a man's ego?"

Their bodies were barely touching, but Serena felt as if he'd stolen all the air from her lungs. "I believe I've heard that somewhere."

"So, how about repairing some of the damage you've done here today?" He lowered his head. "You can't just send me back out into the world without my self-esteem." His lips were a whisper away from Serena's. All she had to do was go up on her toes just the slightest bit. "I'd never survive."

"You're impossible," she breathed as his mouth covered hers.

Serena could feel his smile against her lips. "I know."

No one could call it a kiss. Soft as angel wings, gentle as a summer breeze, it was more of a whisper than a proper kiss. Meltingly soft and caressingly delicate, it had the effect of turning her knees to water. A white light curled through her body, rivaling the brilliant yellow sun for warmth. Serena's fingers tightened on his as her needs rose, hot and primitive.

Across the deep gully, the panther roared; somewhere deep in the recesses of the zoo an African elephant trumpeted. Birds from a nearby aviary filled the air with their songs and at a snack bar a hundred feet away a group of schoolchildren noisily called out their orders. But Serena was oblivious to anything but the tender pressure of Alex's lips as they moved tantalizingly from one corner of her mouth to the other.

"This was a good idea." Alex lifted his head to look down at her. Lord, how he loved the polished pewter shade her eyes took on when she was aroused. "Remind me the next time I want to have my way with you to bring you to the panther exhibit."

Was the ground spinning, or was it her? "That may be a little difficult," Serena managed to say. "I leave for France next week."

"Wrong."

A cold fist twisted Serena's heart. *Oh, no,* she begged him silently. *Please don't ask me not to go. Don't make me choose.*

"What does that mean?" She shook her hands loose as she backed away from him.

Ice. Cold, smooth and impenetrable. It flowed over her even as he watched. Damn. What would it take before she relaxed her guard around him?

Alex stifled a frustrated sigh as he tugged on her hair. He was back on the defensive, but he had yet to serve his ace. "It means, my love, that there's been a change in plans. We're leaving for France tomorrow."

Her eyes narrowed. "We? As in you and I?"

He glanced around. "See anyone else around here who qualifies?"

Serena's fingers curled around the railing. She shook her head. "I can't go to France with you."

"Can't? Or won't?" Alex's eyes gleamed like jet in the bright sun. His point. He waited patiently for Serena's return.

When Serena didn't think she could stand another moment of Alex's silent scrutiny, she turned her gaze out over the moat. The panther had resumed its back-and-forth pacing, watching them with unblinking yellow eyes.

"What are you afraid of, Serena?" Alex taunted softly.

His words had the effect of stiffening her spine, strengthening her resolve, clearing her head. "Nothing." She turned to look at him, meeting his oddly gentle gaze with a level one of her own. "I'm not afraid of anything. Or anyone," she tacked on as she read the unspoken question in his eyes.

She had played his game. Precisely as planned. *Match point.* "Then there's no problem, is there?" He cupped her softly distressed face with his hand. "Think of it, Serena. Paris in the springtime. You and I strolling the Champs Élysés, drinking wine in some quaint little sidewalk café, making slow, passionate love."

His fingers took hold of her wrist, detecting the sudden leap of her pulse. His eyes smiled down at her. "I'll bet you've never been to the Champ-de-Mars," he guessed, remember-

ing what she had said about sight-seeing taking up too much
time during tournaments.

When she shook her head, Alex grinned. "You'll love it. It
used to be a military training ground. Now it's a lovely green
park, with carousels and donkey rides and puppet shows."

The triumphant smile should have irritated her, but for
some reason it didn't. What he was suggesting admittedly
sounded like heaven. Fools rush in, Serena thought as she
made her decision.

"I'll go," she said with a soft sigh of surrender.

Alex's head swooped down to plant a quick, hard kiss
against her lips. "You won't regret it," he promised huskily.
His ebony eyes swept over her face. "Paris was made for a
woman like you."

She linked her fingers through his, pulling him away from
the exhibit. "It was the puppet show that did it," she alleged
blithely. "Come on, Alex, I'll buy you some popcorn."

Serena reminded Alex of a wide-eyed child as she dragged
him from one corner of the National Zoo to the other. She
thought the baby elephants darling, oohed and ahed with the
rest of the tourists over the pandas from China and clung to
his arm as they toured the reptile house. Her response caused
Alex to decide that, next to the panther, he liked the reptile
exhibit the best.

"I've come to a decision," Serena said after he had finally
convinced her to take a break. They were seated on a bench
in a grove of leafy trees in a secluded area away from the main
part of the zoo.

Alex put his arm around her shoulders and smiled down
at her. "About what?"

"I absolutely adore cotton candy." She tore off another
piece of the sticky spun confection. "I think it's all I'm going
to eat from now on."

"I'll be surprised if you can ever eat again. So far today
you've gone through two boxes of popcorn, a hot dog with

everything on it, three orange sodas, a bag of peanuts and now that stuff." He eyed the pink candy dubiously.

Serena sighed happily. She had admittedly gone off her training diet, just for today. And had enjoyed every moment of it. "It's been wonderful. Who would have suspected that you could get such delicious food at a zoo?" She smiled up at him. "Do they have a zoo in Paris?"

"Lots of them."

"Good. Promise me that we'll visit them all?" she asked as she licked her fingers.

Alex took her hand and brought it to his lips. He took her fingers into the dark recesses of his mouth one by one, his swirling tongue gathering in the sweet, sticky candy. She could have protested; she could have pulled away. But as his mouth and lips conspired to liquefy her bones, Serena found herself caught in a silver snare of desire, unable to resist.

"If we have time," he agreed huskily. "As enjoyable as this has been, there are a few other things I had in mind to do." His lips moved to the center of her palm, where his tongue traced slow, lazy circles.

"If we have time," she echoed, sinking against the back of the wooden bench as her spine seemed to melt.

How did he do it? How could such a simple, nonthreat ening gesture cause her to feel as if she were sinking into quicksand? Seeking to escape the intensity of his dark knowing gaze, Serena closed her eyes. The image of a cruel black panther swirled up behind her lids. Dangerous, she re minded herself. So, so dangerous.

Alex was aware of the precise moment of Serena's change in mood. Her body was an uncannily accurate barometer of her mind. Her hand went cold; her back stiffened to the strength of steel. Tension radiated from every sun-warmed pore. He stifled the urge to shake her.

"We'd better get going, we both have some packing to do," he said conversationally even as he fought a savage urge to drag her off into the bushes and make love to her until she realized that she couldn't live without him.

"About that . . ." Serena faltered, attempting to find some graceful way out of the trip she was suddenly dreading.

His eyes abruptly turned hard, possessing the steely strength of flint. "Uh-uh. I'm not letting you back out of it that easily, sweetheart. We had a deal. You promised to see Paris with me and I'm going to hold you to it."

She lifted her chin, her gaze as frosty as the mechanically cooled air of the polar-bear exhibit. "You can't force me to go with you," she pointed out, feeling a little safer as a family, obviously tourists from their identical "Where the hell is Tortilla Flats?" T-shirts, came around the corner.

His fingers curled around her shoulders. "Want to bet?"

Anger. It flared, hot and unrestrained, steamrollering over passions far more dangerous. Bathed in the sensual glow of the past few hours, Serena had forgotten Alex's ability to trigger her temper.

"Just what are you going to do?" she challenged. "Tie me up and toss me in the baggage compartment with your luggage?"

Cheeks that were pale as driven snow only moments before flared crimson. Glacial eyes now shot sparks. And her body, which had been rigid and forbidding, practically quivered with barely restrained indignation. She was one hell of a woman, Alex considered. And after last night, whether Serena would admit it or not, she was his woman.

"You know," he drawled, "now that you've mentioned it, that's not such a bad idea. It'd save me the price of one seat on the Concorde."

Before she could discern his intentions, Alex had scooped her up and slung her over his shoulder. "Twisted her ankle," he explained cheerily to the open-mouthed tourists who stepped off the narrow path to allow him to pass.

"When we get back to the hotel, I'm going to kill you," Serena hissed.

"When we get back to the hotel," Alex corrected amiably, "we're going to make love."

PARIS BY DAY. The white Basilique du Sacré-Coeur rising into the sky. The Louvre. Long, leisurely walks, hand in hand, along the boulevards. Children sailing toy boats in the central pool of Luxembourg Gardens on the left bank of the Seine. Punch and Judy shows. Shopping at the Galeries Lafayette. Soft, sweet springtime rains.

Paris by night. The Eiffel Tower, Notre Dame, the Arc de Triomphe, the Place de la Concorde, all basking in the gleam of hundreds of spotlights. Laughter. Couples strolling arm in arm, stopping in the shadows to steal a kiss. Still more laughter. Sweet, lingering lovemaking.

Serena gave herself up to all the city—and Alex—had to offer, feeling like Rip Van Winkle as she viewed this new and glorious world for what seemed to be the first time. She had never been happier. Alex's presence made even the grueling daily practice sessions enjoyable.

Two weeks after arriving in the city, Serena was in the final set of the French Open. As a sporting event, the match rivaled a Beethoven symphony for depth, subtlety and complexity.

Serena brushed her blond bangs off her forehead as she prepared to serve. Her white shoes, as well as her dress, bore blood-red smudges from the clay. Her arm throbbed and her throat was bone dry. Serena had been facing Gabriella Dupree across that net for what seemed like days, although it was only a little over three hours. Whenever she thought she had her on the ropes, the young woman came back with a shot that caused the crowd to cheer wildly. Despite the fact that Serena was playing a Frenchwoman, in the French capital, the fans appeared evenly divided. At this point they were willing to cheer anything or anyone that would permit the record-setting match to continue.

"That last rally took fifty-two strokes," Marty Jennings muttered to Alex, as the two men sat side by side in the friends' box. "If Serena was looking for the ultimate test for her arm, she's definitely found it this afternoon."

"She'll take it," Alex said, his gaze glued to Serena's face.

Her expression was unreadable, but he knew that at this moment she was probably more alive than she had ever been. Including, he conceded reluctantly, when they were making love. She was playing for all the marbles; he couldn't imagine her walking off the court without the championship. She'd wanted it, worked for it too long to give up now. She was beautiful, he considered, not for the first time certainly, as he watched her dive to return a crosscourt backhand. Part princess, part prizefighter. The woman he loved.

Alex had admitted that fact to himself long enough ago to have grown comfortable with the idea. After Carly's stunning accusation, he had been forced to reexamine his feelings. By the time he had made love to Serena that first time in Washington, he had suspected Carly might have called this one right. By the next morning, Alex had known for sure.

He had not yet confided this momentous fact to Serena, telling himself that he wanted to give her time to get used to the idea. In truth, he had not been at all sure how she would take the news. Knowing that their future was inexorably entangled with her career comeback, Alex had decided not to tell her until after Wimbledon. But, damn, the wait was driving him crazy. *Patience*, he reminded himself.

A Gallic pout formed on Gabriella's lips as she mishit the ball into the net. She swished back to the baseline, displaying ruffled panties beneath her minuscule skirt. The men in the grandstand roared their approval. Serena didn't blink as she bent down, awaiting Gabriella's serve.

Twenty minutes later Serena was inwardly wilting like edelweiss in a hothouse. Outwardly, she remained calm, forgoing the displays of temper Gabriella was exhibiting more with each passing volley. She could outlast her, Serena told herself. All she had to do was continue to play the percentage shots and not opt for anything fancy. She sprinkled water on her racket grip during the changeover to cool it off, then wiped it dry with a towel. She looked up at the friends' box. Her gray eyes, as they smiled appreciatively at Alex's thumbs-up sign, did not reveal that her legs had turned to water two games ago.

The crowd groaned in unison as Serena faulted. Reminding herself that she was only as good as her second serve, Serena took a deep breath. She uncoiled into the ball, hitting a severe kick serve that had Gabriella sliding on the red clay in a rash attempt to save the point. Serena served again. Gabriella managed a good return, but with her uncanny ability to foresee where a shot was heading, Serena was waiting for it. She sent a hard forehand drive shimmering down the line, far to Gabriella's left. The Frenchwoman lunged at it, but the ball spun low off her backhand into the net. The crowd roared.

Alex's voice was harsh and strained as he cheered Serena on. She was fighting like a tiger, not giving up a thing. She was strong, powerful, vibrant. Yet after each point, Serena's Ice Princess image would immediately resurface. She'd raise her head as if an invisible crown were being placed on it, stare straight ahead and walk immediately back to position.

Only when she finally ended the grueling contest by climbing an invisible ladder to reach for a lob that she drove crosscourt to blaze by Gabriella did Serena allow a slight smile to curve her lips. Walking off the court after shaking hands with a perspiration-drenched opponent, Serena couldn't help wondering if somehow her father was watching. She knew that even the perfectionist William Lawrence would have been forced to approve of her performance to-day.

THE PARTY WAS IN FULL SWING when Serena and Alex arrived. Lindsay lifted a glass of champagne toward Serena. "Congrats. Ya dusted her, ya did."

Serena laughed. "How can you call a match that breaks the record for volleys a dusting?"

Lindsay polished off the sparkling wine, reaching out to replace her glass with a full one from a passing tray. "We Aussies have our own way of lookin' at things." Her brown eyes turned to Alex. "And if I do say so, the scenery 'as definitely improved this year."

He grinned in response. "Alex Bedare," he said, extending a hand. "I've always been a fan of yours, Miss Carlow. It's a pleasure to meet you."

"Call me Lindsay, love," she corrected. "Isn't 'e a right proper bastard," Lindsay remarked to Serena. "Does he always say precisely the right thing?"

"Always," Serena agreed easily, knowing the Australian trait for using expletives as terms of affection.

"Let me take a look at you, mate." Lindsay slowly walked around Alex as if he were a prize bull she was contemplating purchasing. "You're a fine one, you are," she said, sipping the effervescent champagne. "Tell me, my sheikh of the burning sands, 'as the princess here staked her claim? Or are you up for grabs?"

Serena shook her head good-naturedly. "How many of those have you had?"

Lindsay stared at the now empty glass in her hand. "Who counts? Besides, it's your fault. After watchin' that bloomin' match go on and on, I was dry enough to spit chips." She grinned crookedly at Serena. "It's a party, duchess. Everyone's allowed to be a bit of a dero, right?" she asked Alex.

"Dero?" he asked blankly.

He'd been managing to keep up with Lindsay's Australian failure to enunciate, but the additional alcohol she had obviously consumed had made her slur her words. His difficulty in comprehending was also compounded by the fact that Lindsay had lapsed into a delightful, distorted form of the English language called Strine. A colorful combination of cockney and Australian English, the words emerged in a rush.

"Neighborhood drunk," Serena translated. "You'll have to excuse my friend. The rumor that Australians speak English is highly exaggerated."

"What do you expect? We walk alone hanging from the bottom of the world," Lindsay said. "We're entitled to our own lingo, aren't we, mate?" She smiled up at Alex.

"Sounds fair enough to me," he said with an answering grin.

Lindsay rocked back on her heels. "There's a question I've been dyin' to ask you for weeks."

"Shoot," Alex agreed amiably.

"Don't encourage her," Serena said.

Lindsay ignored her friend's warning tone. "Are you two as serious as you look? Or is this just a Paris-in-springtime fling?"

"We're serious," Alex answered immediately.

"It's just a fling," Serena said at the same time.

The dance band in the corner chose that precise moment to stop playing. As the heavy silence swirled around them, Lindsay's brown eyes moved from Serena to Alex and back again.

"Well," she said finally, "it looks as if you two have some talking to do." She gave Serena a hug. "Congrats again on the match, love. I enjoyed watching that bloody sheila get her comeuppance."

She lowered her voice, her drawled words intended only for Serena's ears. "You're a drongo if you let this one get away." With that, Lindsay gave Alex a big smile before wandering off into the crowd, her gait anything but steady.

"What did she say to you?" he asked.

"She said I was an idiot," Serena murmured absently, her mind still focused on Alex's stunning statement.

What did he mean, it was serious? She had agreed to come to Paris with him to sample whatever life had to offer. It had been an extemporaneous act, rashly conceived, just as rashly acted upon. He had urged her to live for the moment. That was precisely what she was doing. No past. No future. Those were the rules of the game they had been playing from the beginning.

Alex stopped himself from agreeing with Lindsay's observation, not wanting to ruin Serena's evening with an argument. He had vowed to wait until after Wimbledon for the showdown he knew was inevitable. And wait he would. But damn, it was going to be the most difficult thing he'd ever done.

All afternoon, as he had watched Serena struggle back, time and time again, never conceding a point, he had wanted to stand up and shout out his love for her. But he'd held his tongue. As he did now.

"Let's dance." He put his hand on her back and led her onto the dance floor.

"What did you mean back there?" she asked, automatically putting her arms around his neck.

Alex nuzzled her ear. "Back where?" he murmured. "God, you smell good. Like springtime. Meadows in bloom, soft yellow sunshine . . ."

His hands, resting lightly just below her waist, and his deep voice were conspiring to make Serena forget her original question. She struggled against the rising tide of desire.

"Why did you tell Lindsay that we were serious?" she asked shakily as his teeth nibbled at her earlobe.

"It seemed like the right thing to say at the time," he answered casually. "Serena?"

Her mind was floating, out of reach on a shimmering plane. "Hmm?"

"I'm not up on tennis protocol," he admitted. "How long do the winners have to hang around the victory ball?" His palms slipped lower, pressing her against him, allowing her to feel the extent of his desire.

"Speaking as the victor, I'd say we've been here long enough." Looking up at him, Serena's eyes gleamed with sensuous invitation.

She could feel his chuckle. "I always knew you were a winner, Serena Lawrence." He gave her a hard, possessive kiss before walking with her toward the door.

Much later that night, Serena secretly admitted that there were things far more thrilling, worlds more satisfying than winning a tennis tournament. Even one as important as the French Open.

12

WIMBLEDON. The Lawn Tennis Championships. The smell of roses and newly mown grass, the taste of champagne and dripping ice lollies. Hallowed acres—the grass, the grandstands, the ivy over the grandstands, even the low hedges bordering the fourteen field courts south of Centre Court—were all dark green. But there were other colors as well: flower boxes overflowing with pink and blue hydrangeas brought in for the Wimbledon fortnight, the crimson uniforms of the Wimbledon band, the scarlet of strawberries, the white of rich Devonshire cream. Wimbledon. The British utter it in the same reverent tones they use for Trafalgar.

To emerge at Wimbledon is to be written into history for all time. To win Wimbledon is to win the world championship. In the same way that little boys who want to grow up to be football players dream of the Super Bowl and Little Leaguers dream of the World Series, children the world over who want to be tennis players dream of Wimbledon.

Garden parties. Elizabethan drama. An annual two-week carnival. A tennis tournament. Wimbledon is all this. And more.

Serena no longer cared that she had been forced to play three preliminary rounds to qualify. She was here. That was all that mattered.

"I love it here," she said softly, holding Alex's hand as she thought how pretty the black shadows from the grandstand looked on the thick green grass.

The lush greenery made it cozy while the perfect geometry of the courts gave her a nice feeling. Unlike Forest Hills.

Serena had always hated playing in the U.S. Open. The fences, angled to the baseline, always threw her game off. Here, however, the hedges, the grass courts, even the upholstered green chairs in the Royal Box were all a silent tribute to British precision.

"I love everything about Wimbledon."

"If the British press is any example, Wimbledon loves you back," Alex said. "You're one of the few players that they haven't taken a swipe at."

"I've been lucky. Besides, the English love upsets; they'll always root for the underdog."

She put her arm in his as they strolled the Tea Lawn. Things were quiet now, but in twenty-four hours the gates of the All-England Lawn Tennis and Croquet Club would swing open and the peaceful serenity would be replaced by an aura more accurately described as resembling bedlam.

Alex noticed that Serena had left unsaid the fact that *she* was the decided underdog, despite her wins in Italy, France and in the qualifying rounds at Eastbourne. The odds at the London bookmakers were twenty to one against her lasting through the quarter finals.

"Nervous?"

As her eyes swept the sunbaked stone tiers on either side of the stadium, envisioning them filled with cheering fans, Serena tried to put her feelings into words.

"Edgy," she decided. "But the good kind of nervousness that comes from anticipation. Not fear."

He squeezed her fingers reassuringly. "You'll do fine."

"Fine isn't good enough. I need to win," she said heatedly. "I intend to win."

Alex's dark eyes were suddenly solemn. "Whatever you do, love," he said quietly, "make certain that you're doing it for yourself."

"What exactly does that mean?" she asked stiffly.

Not now, Alex warned himself. *You've waited this long.* He could wait two more weeks. A fortnight. Fourteen short days. It seemed forever.

"Come on," he said suddenly. "We're going to be spending enough time around here beginning tomorrow."

"Where are we going?"

"What would you like to do?"

Serena thought for a moment. "I want to do everything I've never had time to do."

"I'm afraid you're going to have to be a bit more explicit," he said with a smile.

"All right. I want to ride on one of those cute double-decker buses, I want to go to Madame Tussaud's, watch the changing of the guard at Buckingham Palace, visit Westminister Abbey, Covent Gardens, The Tower of London—"

"Whoa." Alex held up his hand. "You spent the majority of your life in England. Didn't you ever do any of those things?"

"I was busy," she murmured, not wanting to admit that the few times she hadn't been practicing, her father had vetoed any sight-seeing trips. William Lawrence had always abhorred crowds. Thinking back on it, Serena could recall very few individuals her father had approved of.

"You can't expect to do a lifetime of catching up in one afternoon, sweetheart."

"I suppose it is a bit unrealistic." Serena wanted to sigh but managed a smile instead.

"Just a bit," he agreed. "Why don't you let me make a suggestion?"

She hesitated only a moment. "Fine."

"A picnic at Kensington Gardens. Then a tour of the zoo."

Serena beamed her approval. "Will they have cotton candy?"

He ran a hand down her hair. "How could they not?"

SERENA STOOD IN FRONT of the statue of Peter Pan in Kensington Gardens. "I always loved that story," she said softly. "My father took me to see it once, on my seventh birthday. He didn't really want to go, but I begged and begged." A reminiscent smile quirked at the corners of her lips. "When that didn't work, I threw a tantrum."

"And that did it?"

She shook her head. "No, that was what almost got my tennis racket taken away for a week."

Alex refrained from saying that particular punishment could have been a blessing in disguise.

"Anyway," she continued, her face flushed with the long-ago memory, "it seemed like magic. I never wanted it to end."

Desire flowed lazily through him as he observed the sunshine glinting off Serena's hair. He had been right about the texture from the start. It felt like pure silk to the touch.

"I can see you as a little girl, with wide believing gray eyes, clapping for Tinker Bell to come alive."

Serena's hand turned cold in his. "It was a long time ago," she murmured distractedly. "I can't remember the details."

She was a rotten liar, Alex determined. But a beautiful one. A distant shadow moved across her eyes, saying more than words ever could. Alex realized that William Lawrence, in his goal to create a clone of himself, had not permitted the child Serena to believe in fairies. He didn't believe it an accident that her favorite childhood story was about a little boy who did not want to grow up; it was readily apparent that Serena had never been allowed any type of childhood.

He brushed his lips against her hair. "Ready to try out the zoo?"

She leaned against him, closing her eyes, drawing from the comfort he offered. Alex heard her sigh and felt her slowly relax as his hands moved gently on her back. They remained that way for a long, silent moment. Finally, Serena tilted her head back to look up at him. Her silver eyes were eloquent in their desire.

"I'd rather go back to the hotel. I need you, Alex."

At this moment, she could have asked Alex for anything imaginable and he would have moved heaven and earth to get it. That she was admitting her need so openly, without feminine guile, without excuses, tore at the fragile thread of his self-restraint. His arms tightened around her, as if he was afraid she'd vanish like some ethereal spirit who dwelt only in his fantasies.

I love you, his desperate mind cried out. *God, how I love you, Serena Lawrence!* "We can be there in fifteen minutes," he said instead.

Her relief was palpable as she began walking with him out of the gardens. "Fifteen minutes," she echoed. "Is that all?"

He stopped in his tracks to cover her mouth with his. Her enticing feminine scent swam in his head. Passion rose inside him, threatening to do away with any vestiges of civilization. He wanted her warm and naked underneath him. He needed to feel her flesh like flaming satin against his skin; he longed to hear the soft little cries she made; he wanted her hands to stroke his body as he would caress hers until all control had disintegrated. Alex ached for Serena with every fiber of his being.

"Believe me," he said as he forced himself to release her avid mouth, "it's going to be the longest fifteen minutes of my life."

THE TENSION GENERATED by Wimbledon was palpable. It was in the air as all of London became caught up in the spirit of the fortnight. The windows of Harrods were decorated with tennis dresses; the underground trains to Southfields, the Wimbledon subway stop, were packed each day with fans carrying picnic hampers. The radio shows talked of little else, each host and hostess fighting tooth and nail as they vied for a full-fledged star to interview on the air. When a bout of influenza sped through the dressing rooms, striking high and low seeds alike, the struggle for celebrity guests heightened.

By the middle of the second week, Serena caved in to the continual pressure, granting one of the less obnoxious radio hosts an interview.

"You're playing in the semifinals," the man said, telling her nothing that she did not already know. "Are you surprised that you've made it this far?"

Serena smiled sweetly, despite the fact that her audience would only be hearing her voice. "I'm pleased that I've been playing well, but I'm not really surprised. After all, I've been working for this a very long time."

This time her smile was genuine. "As pleased as I am with my wins, I'm especially happy that I've been able to give the fans some good games to watch. I've always loved Wimbledon; there's something larger than life about it. All the pomp and circumstance—it's like grand opera at its best."

Alex, sitting in the control booth with the engineer, could practically hear listeners all over the country sighing in unison. He wasn't the only one who could turn a diplomatic phrase when called upon to do so. He sent Serena an appreciative grin.

"And yet," the interviewer continued doggedly, "grass has never been your best surface."

"Grass is fluky: in the past I've preferred clay," Serena admitted easily. "The lengthy volleys suited my style of play."

"Well, you certainly had a few drawn-out volleys in the French Open," he reminded the listeners. "What was that one point? Fifty strokes?"

"Fifty-two."

The bored engineer drew in a breath, eyeing Serena with renewed interest and not a little admiration.

"Despite your expected success on the Italian and French clay, we've recently seen some distinct changes in your game. Will you continue this more aggressive style of play?"

"I suppose I have altered my style of play a bit," she allowed. "I've been charging the net more than I used to. So long as it doesn't rain and the grass stays dry, I probably won't change anything."

"The word around town is that the Ice Dolly is melting." He called her by the name the British press had tagged on her years earlier, a reference to the ice lollie, a popular Wimbledon treat.

"We all grow up," she said, exchanging a long glance with Alex.

They both knew she had been allowing her emotions to come to the surface more. To Serena's surprise, instead of interfering with her game, it had helped her, keeping her adrenaline high, her senses well-honed. While she hadn't begun arguing calls, an arched brow or an upward glance toward the heavens had gotten her displeasure across succinctly. In the past, the Ice Princess would not have allowed even that show of temperament.

"It's rumored that a romance is brewing. Can we expect an announcement soon?"

Serena had always understood that her chosen career left her personal life open to conjecture. She had long accepted the fact that she was on public display. She shared her talent; her fans gave applause and recognition. It was not that different from being an actress.

In the beginning, she had been written about not so much because she was a tennis player but because she was young and also realized that a vast number of those fans wanted her to stay the same little girl. Something she could no longer do, even if she wanted to. Which she didn't. If nothing else came of her relationship with Alex, he had held up a mirror, forcing her to view Serena Lawrence as she really was. Not some tennis-playing machine, but a woman. With a woman's capacity for passion. For that Serena would always be grateful.

"I'd rather not discuss my personal life," she finally answered the question with a soft smile. "I'm sure you can understand."

The flash of irritation that sparked in his eyes indicated that the man did not understand at all. But he was not about to attack Serena Lawrence. Not when each day's victory gained her additonal supporters. As much as he'd like to pursue the question of the Ice Dolly and the diplomat, the man wanted to keep his job even more.

"How do you respond to those individuals who say that women don't belong in Center Court?" he asked, changing tactics. "That it's the men the fans really come to see?"

Serena combed her fingers through her hair as she chose her words carefully. It was a long-argued topic. One that had always annoyed her considerably.

"Admittedly, women's tennis looks easy," she began slowly. "Compared to the men's game, the average viewer sees it in the same way he might look at football and golf.

"A man watching a football game doesn't picture himself wearing a defensive lineman's jersey because the physical gap is too wide. But when he's watching Jack Nicklaus sink a perfect putt, he puts himself in Jack's shoes.

"In the same way, fans watch the men play tennis and marvel at their speed and power. Then they turn around and watch our control and believe anyone can do it." Her smile sounded in her voice. "But believe me, it's a lot harder than it looks."

She sat back, breathing a silent sigh as the interviewer made his closing statement. Soon she was wrapped in Alex's arms in the back of the limousine.

"You were terrific." He pressed his lips to hers.

"The driver," Serena complained, pressing her palms against Alex's chest as she cast a glance upward into the rearview mirror.

"Is paid to drive." He caught her bottom lip between his teeth.

Desire swirled up, stunning her with its intensity. She had known Alex for almost three months; they had been lovers for six weeks. She would have expected the hunger to lessen as familiarity set in. Instead, she found herself wanting him with a passion that frightened her whenever she allowed herself to contemplate its fury. Every time he looked at her, touched his lips to hers, caressed her, Serena felt as if she were flung headlong into a hurricane.

She tilted her head back, breaking the heated contact. "You frighten me at times," she whispered.

Alex's fingers tightened around her waist. *Easy,* he warned himself. *Don't press.* They were coming down to the wire now. Tomorrow's semifinal match and then the final on Centre Court. Then he and Serena were going to get married.

"I thought we had established that I'd never hurt you."

"We did," she said a little too quickly. His mouth was so close, so tempting. Serena knew that no mater how many times she kissed Alex, it would never be enough.

His eyes skimmed over her face. "Perhaps I'm missing something. But I don't understand."

"I'm afraid of my feelings for you," she blurted out, tears stinging behind her lids. Tears that she resolutely blinked away. She was not so far gone that she'd let anyone, even Alex, see her cry. That was one intimacy she could never allow. "I feel so out of control when I'm with you."

"And you think I don't?" he asked gruffly. "Do you have any idea how difficult it is for me to be with you in public, to make polite small talk and nod and smile and say the proper things, when all I can think about is going back to our room and undressing you. Touching you. Kissing you. Feeling those firm, tanned legs around my hips."

Just his words had her body softening in response. "That's what I'm talking about," she complained. "Feel this." She grabbed his hand and placed it over her breast.

His fingers flexed appreciatively. "Mmm, nice."

"I meant my heart, damn it." It was the first time Alex had ever heard her curse, which indicated how honestly distressed Serena really was. "It beats all crazy like this whenever I'm with you."

"So?" He pressed her palm against the hard wall of his chest, where Serena felt his heart beating with an identical rapid rhythm. "That's what makes it good, Serena. Perhaps logic can't explain how I feel about you, and perhaps you can't analyze why the world tilts a little on its axis whenever we come together. But you can't deny that it isn't good, love. Very, very good."

His lips brushed over hers, his dark mustache feathering her skin with a silky, provocative touch.

"No," she said with a rippling sigh. "I can't."

He buried his face in her hair, breathing in the scent of wild flowers. Every cell in his body cried out the need to tell her he loved her. Here. Now. But a little voice in the back of his mind counseled restraint. Alex closed his eyes and viewed his father's gentle features. *Patience*.

His fingers were far from steady as he cupped her chin, tilting her head back to meet his loving gaze. "We've been happy together, Serena. Let's just leave it at that for now."

For now. His words struck at her like a lash. Serena forced herself to remember that she was the one who had no use for long-term involvements. Her life was tennis. Alex was a delightful interlude. But he was merely that. An interlude. Once these golden days of summer had given way to the crisp tang of autumn, he would be gone. Back to his classroom. That was precisely what she wanted. Wasn't it?

"For now," she agreed breathlessly. Flinging her arms around his neck, Serena pressed her desperate lips to his.

DESPITE A NAGGING HEADACHE, Serena won the match the following day, 7-5, 2-6, 6-2. As she walked from the court, she was swept into a pair of strong arms.

"Donovan!" she cried out happily. "How long have you been here?"

He grinned down at her. "Long enough to watch you hit your way into the finals. What was it with that woman, anyway? One minute she reminded me of Camille, grabbing her stomach, looking like she was going to keel over at any second. Then on the next point, she'd be running like a gazelle."

"She could have the flu," Serena said, wanting to give Karla Mueller the benefit of the doubt. "It *was* distracting, though."

"Flu, hell," Alex accused as he came up behind Donovan. "She was trying to throw you off."

Serena lifted her face for his kiss. "That's what I love about you, Alex. You're so impartial. Did you know Donovan was coming?"

"Sure."

"Why didn't you tell me?"

"Because he swore me to secrecy. Your brother wanted to surprise you, sweetheart."

"Men," Serena muttered. "Sometimes I think you all belong to one great fraternity, the way you stick together."

"It's the one way we can survive," Alex said easily.

She shot an accusing glance Donovan's way. "Terrific. Now you're getting together to rehearse each other's lines. I've got to shower and change. And meet the reporters in the press room." She went up on her toes to kiss Donovan's bearded cheek. "You are having dinner with us, aren't you?"

Donovan's appraising green eyes slid to Alex. "That'd be great. If I wouldn't be in the way."

"In the way? My best girl's brother?" Alex asked, lifting a black brow. "Never."

"We can't take you out on the town," Serena apologized.

"I'll probably survive," Donovan said dryly. "After all, I didn't fly all the way across the United States, then the Atlantic Ocean to go to a party with a bunch of people I don't even know."

"I have to be in bed early," she explained. "I'm playing in the finals tomorrow."

"Hey, runt, even I couldn't forget a thing like that." Donovan's expression was clearly wounded.

Alex leaned down to give Serena a quick peck on the cheek. "As for getting to bed early," he said on a low, husky note, "sweetheart, you've read my mind."

13

"HEY, SERENA, GOOD LUCK against Fleming tomorrow."

Despite a throbbing headache, Serena smiled as a slim red-haired man stopped by their table.

"You, too," she said, knowing that Phillip Greene represented Great Britain's hope to wrest the title away from Keith Larson, an eighteen-year-old American who had been seeded first in the tournament.

Serena introduced Phillip to Alex, who won points by congratulating the tennis player on winning his fifty-fifth Grand Prix singles title in Stockholm. Serena was not particularly surprised by Alex's knowledge. Throughout the weeks in Paris and London, she had seen him display an amazing amount of trivial information. When she had questioned him about it, he'd shrugged it off, saying he was accustomed to doing his homework before having to make cocktail-party conversation. The casual remark had reminded her that, while he appeared to be a man interested solely in enjoying life to the fullest, he was no stranger to hard work.

Donovan and Phillip had met before at other tournaments. The two men shook hands and exchanged pleasantries.

"I know that as an American, I should be rooting for Keith," Serena said, "but to tell you the truth, I'm beginning to get a Methuselah complex. I'd like to see us old folks win. Not that thirty is old," Serena hastened to add, remembering that Phillip had celebrated his birthday just last week.

Pulling up a chair, he joined them momentarily. "It's different these days. When we were coming up, people saw tennis as a craft. Something you work on and perfect over the course of years. And years." He frowned. "Today you either prove yourself a natural by winning Wimbledon when you're a teenager, or you're just another face in the crowd."

"Keith's a one-dimensional player," Serena offered encouragingly. "He relies too heavily on that lethal forehand of his."

"They should have pulled him off the tour for six months to teach him to volley," Phillip agreed. "I'm hoping that'll prove his downfall." As if he realized he was putting a damper on an otherwise enjoyable evening, Phillip shook his head and shrugged. "Oh, well, what's that they say about times a-changing?"

"They say it keeps things interesting," Serena answered with a smile.

"Speaking of changes, I've noticed some in your game. In the olden days, the only time I saw you come into the net was to accept flowers. When did you start experimenting with that chip-and-charge game?"

"Since I decided it was time to retire the Ice Dolly."

"What does Marty think about this?"

"You know Marty. He doesn't interfere so long as everything's working." Her gray eyes twinkled as she gave him a gamine grin. "However, he did seem a little rattled when these ruby-red lips muttered a swear word during practice yesterday."

Phillip laughed appreciatively as he rose from the chair and extended his hand to Alex. "I've got a feeling you have something to do with Serena's metamorphosis," he said. "Congratulations. From one who's been caught in her ice flow."

"I wasn't that bad," Serena protested.

Phillip bent down and gave her a quick peck on the cheek. "Honey, half the guys on the tour struck out with you over the years."

"What about the other half?" Donovan asked interestedly, ignoring Serena's warning glare.

Phillip's laugh was rich and full-bodied. "The other half never worked up the nerve to try." After wishing Serena good luck again, he was gone.

"Ridiculous conversation," Serena muttered, rubbing her temples with her fingertips. "Here we are, in one of the world's most interesting cities, at the premier of tennis tournaments, and all you men can find to talk about is my love life." She turned resolutely to Donovan. "So tell me, how's Gloria?"

"As we speak, Gloria is undoubtedly watching 'Miami Vice.' That is, if her set's still working. It's been on the blink lately; I'm afraid it's going to go out entirely."

"I wouldn't want to be around when that happens," Alex offered. "She's bound to hit the roof."

Donovan lifted his pint of lager to his lips. "Don't worry," he said casually. "I've got a contingency plan."

Serena and Alex exchanged a curious look. It was not like Donovan to behave so offhandedly about any of his gorillas. And Gloria was obviously his favorite.

"A contingency plan?" Serena asked.

Donovan's green eyes danced with laughter. "I figure Alex can keep her sufficiently entertained until the set gets back from the shop."

Alex lifted his hands. "Not me, pal. I still haven't gotten over the last time you stuck me in with her. I could have been killed."

"Gloria likes you," Donovan argued.

"I suppose she told you that."

He inclined his head. "In a way. She keeps making the sign for guitar. She doesn't seem to be able to distinguish between a guitar and a ukulele," he apologized.

"Terrific," Alex countered, "so let Springsteen serenade her next time you need a diversion."

After the shared laughter, Donovan braced his elbows on the table and turned to Serena. "You've never played Kathy Fleming, have you?"

She shook her head then wished she hadn't as the fiendish little man inside with the jackhammer began pounding all the harder. "Uh-uh. She's one of the new kids on the block. While I was stuck in that rehabilitative center, she was working her way up to third seed." Serena had the good grace to grimace slightly. "That sounded like sour grapes, didn't it?"

Donovan smiled understandingly. "A little."

Serena sighed. "Well, anyway, she was out with the flu for the French Open, and instead of Rome she opted for the quick bucks in some indoor match in Canada."

"Haven't you seen her play here?" Donovan asked.

"We've been scheduled for the same match times. I did watch her warm up the other day and got a feel for her strengths and weaknesses. And of course Marty has notebooks full of stuff he's gathered." She managed to smile. "Sometimes I think that man missed his calling. He probably would have been just as happy being a researcher for the *Encyclopaedia Britannica*."

"Marty doesn't seem to take as active an interest in you as some of the other coaches," Alex said, mentioning something that had struck him as curious since first joining Serena on the tour. "I doubt if he's said more than twenty words to you during practice sessions, and during the matches, he's always up in the friends' box with me."

Serena began fiddling nervously with her cutlery. "My father was the kind of coach who watched over my every waking moment. While that might be what a child needs, I think Marty and I have a good arrangement. He's quiet, mellow, and you're right, he hardly says a word. But he's got an amazing eye for what I'm doing right or wrong. And we both understand that he can only walk me as far as the court. From then on, I'm on my own."

Alex opened his mouth to state that perhaps Serena had
been on her own too long. That it was time she allowed
someone else to look out for her, to care for her, to share her
life. He bit the words back before they could make themselves heard. One more night, he reminded himself. In
twenty-four hours, Serena's match would be history. And
then, win or lose, they were going to get on with their life together.

TWO HOURS LATER, Serena and Alex managed to escape to the
privacy of their hotel room. A steady stream of players had
continued by their table, stopping to wish Serena luck and
to trade stories.

"Alone at last," Alex murmured, drawing Serena into his
arms. "I've never been so happy to see anyone as I was Lindsay when she arrived to drag your brother out dancing."

"I thought you liked Donovan."

He smiled beguilingly as he began to unbutton Serena's
blouse. "I do." The scarlet silk fell to the floor as his
palms cupped her breasts. "But I like his sister a great deal better."

"Oh, Alex," Serena whispered as she wrapped her arms
around his neck. "You're going to hate me."

"Never." He was nuzzling her throat as he lowered the zipper on her cotton skirt and pushed it down over her hips.
Serena stepped out of it automatically, only to gasp as his
palms moved up the back of her legs, leaving trails of flame
on her bare skin.

"You are," she murmured achingly. "But not as badly as I'm
going to be hating myself."

Alex put her unexpected resistance down to nervousness
about her finals match tomorrow. He'd just have to use a little diplomatic coaxing. "It's a little late for second thoughts
now, honey."

As his fingers slipped into the waistband of her satiny bikini panties, Serena's body reacted with an answering jolt. Desire warred with pain as her headache raged.

"I'm not having second thoughts," she argued weakly. "You don't understand...."

Something in her voice, desperation that was not feigned, caught Alex's attention. He looked down into her strangely pale face. "What don't I understand, honey?"

Serena managed a weak smile. "I've always hated clichés, but honestly, Alex, I have a blinding headache."

Concern filled his dark eyes. "Have you taken anything?"

"A couple of aspirin, before dinner. But they're not working."

He released her, crossing the room to the bureau, where he took a nightgown from a drawer. He had not been overly surprised to discover that Serena possessed a queen's ransom of silk and lace confections. While her outward behavior would have led one to expect prim, high-necked, virginal white-cotton nightgowns, Alex had known from the beginning that underneath all that ice dwelt a sensual, passionate woman.

"Can you get dressed by yourself?" he asked, putting it into her hands.

"Of course. It's only a headache." Now that she had his full attention, he wondered why he hadn't noticed a lack of color in her cheeks earlier.

"Do you want me to call the switchboard and have them get hold of the tournament doctor?"

"Of course not." She tugged the royal-blue nightgown over her head. The web of powder-blue lace between her breasts was sheer enough to have been spun from glass. Alex suffered a sharp stab of guilt for having such aching desire for a woman who was obviously not at all well. "However, I will take another aspirin if you don't mind."

Grateful for the opportunity to do something, Alex practically ran into the adjoining bathroom, returning with a glass of water and two white tablets.

As she lay in Alex's arms, Serena closed her eyes to the tender touch of his fingers stroking her temples. It was nice to have someone who cared about you, she decided. She had never allowed anyone close enough to experience the pleasure to be found in a warm and loving relationship. Except Donovan, Serena reminded herself. But even then she hadn't allowed him to visit her at the clinic. She was sorry about that, she realized now. She'd been wrong. And she'd hurt him needlessly.

She hadn't realized until sharing this time with Alex that love could not be a part-time emotion. Donovan had loved her and it must have been hell for him to think she didn't return that love. Alex misunderstood Serena's sigh to be one of discomfort and shifted her more comfortably in his arms.

Yes, Serena thought, everything was better for Alex's presence. Paris had been blissful, London delightful, even her match tomorrow gained added significance because he would be in the gallery. As she realized she loved him, Serena didn't panic as she once might have. Instead she smiled. A slow, womanly smile that, had he seen it, would have told him more than words could ever say.

Damn this headache, she swore to herself. If it wasn't for the constant pounding in her head, she'd show Alex exactly how much she loved him. Perhaps it was a romantic streak she was just beginning to discover, but Serena instinctively felt that, as marvelous as their lovemaking had been, admitting her love for him would raise it to exalted heights.

Tomorrow, she decided, wrapping her arms around him as she fit her slender body to his. After the match. Then they'd have the rest of the afternoon and all of the night to explore her theory. The smile stayed on Serena's face long after she had gone to sleep.

"OH, MY GOD, I'm going to die." Serena struggled to sit up in the bed. Lightning bolts flashed inside her head and her stomach was riding a roller coaster.

"Let me get you some more aspirin," Alex suggested, tossing off the sheet as he swung his feet to the floor. "Then I'll call room service for some tea and toast."

At the very mention of food, Serena's stomach roiled. She ran into the bathroom, slamming the door behind her.

"Serena? Are you all right?"

She was seated on the floor, leaning back against the wall. The giant pansies on the wallpaper appeared to be dancing before her eyes.

"Serena?"

She rested her head on her knees, fighting the nausea threatening to rise again in violent waves. "Go away," she mumbled.

"Tell me you're all right," he insisted. Alarm made his voice rough and ragged.

"How can I tell you that when I'm dying?" she argued. "Go away, Alex. Let me go to my grave in peace."

"That does it." He flung open the door and stared down at her. She looked so small crumpled up on the blue-tile floor. So vulnerable.

He tried to think of something—anything—positive to say. "It's raining."

Serena lifted her head and stared up at him with red-rimmed eyes. "Terrific, just what I needed right now. A weather report."

She was allowed to be a little emotional, Alex reminded himself, if what he suspected was true. He might as well get used to it. "I just wanted you to know that it's been coming down all night. They're saying on the radio that the matches will probably have to be delayed. The grounds crew has covered Centre Court."

Centre Court! Her Wimbledon final was today. How on earth could she have forgotten? As she jumped to her feet, white spots swam on a black-velvet background. She started to crumple back to the tile, but Alex was faster, catching her in his arms.

"You need to lie down." He laid her tenderly, almost reverently on the bed. "I'll be right back," he said, his lips brushing her damp forehead. "I'm calling the doctor." Serena tried to mumble an agreement and found she lacked the strength.

Alex had never been so relieved in his life as he was when the doctor finally arrived. Donovan, who had dropped by Serena's room to wish her luck, dragged Alex down to the hotel coffee shop for breakfast at the physician's instructions.

"I should be there with her," Alex fumed over his third cup of coffee. His suspicions over Serena's condition had been replaced by certainty in his mind.

"All you can do is offer comfort," Donovan pointed out all too accurately. "The doctor will be able to give her something to settle her stomach."

"I hope so," Alex muttered, feeling more guilty by the moment.

As his days with Serena had turned into weeks, he had found himself looking more and more forward to having a child. Their child. A little girl with wide gray eyes and blond hair the color of stardust. Never had he taken into account what Serena would have to suffer to give him this child. Alex wondered if she'd ever find it in her heart to forgive him for depriving her of her day on Centre Court.

"I'm going to go up there," he decided, half rising from the booth.

Donovan reached out and caught his arm. "Sit down and finish your eggs."

"I'm not hungry. She might be alone. Needing something. Needing me."

A smile teased at the corners of Donovan's lips. So this was what love did to a man. Turned him into a raving idiot. Donovan was glad he had been spared such grief. Well, there had been one girl, he admitted momentarily, as a memory of golden-brown eyes and sleek chestnut hair flashed into his mind. But that ill-fated college romance had been a very long time ago. He hadn't thought about Brooke Stirling for years. Donovan shook his head to clear it.

"The doctor said he'd call down here when he was finished examining Serena," he reminded Alex patiently. "Give him some time to find out what's wrong."

"I know what's wrong," Alex muttered. "And it's all my fault." He slammed his hand onto the table, causing the silverware to jump in response. Coffee sloshed over the rim of his cup and spread over the table, dripping onto his slacks.

"Damn," he muttered.

Donovan's green eyes displayed curiosity as he handed Alex his napkin. "What's your fault?'

Alex reminded himself that if Serena had wanted her brother to know of her condition, she would have told him herself. Besides, with the frantic pace of the tournament, they hadn't had an opportunity to discuss it themselves. Alex realized that he wasn't the only one waiting for Wimbledon to be over. Obviously Serena had decided to break the news to him once her comeback was established.

It had crossed Alex's mind as he had sat in the booth, drinking coffee he didn't want and hadn't tasted, that there was an outside chance Serena was afraid to tell him. That she wasn't sure what his reaction would be.

Despite his vow to wait until after her match to reveal his love, Alex decided that fate had obviously stepped in to alter those plans. He'd tell her as soon as they were alone. He smiled at the idea.

"Alex?" Donovan's voice broke into the pleasant daydream he was having of his future family. "You can go back up now. The doctor just called."

"It's about time." Alex rose to his feet in a flash and tossed some bills onto the table. "Look, Donovan," he said hesitatingly, "I know she's your sister, and I can appreciate that you're concerned about her, but would you mind if I had some time alone with Serena?"

Donovan nodded understandingly. "Sure. Good luck," he called out. His words were directed at the other man's back as Alex nearly ran from the coffee shop.

"I've given her an injection," the young man dressed in jeans and running shoes told Alex as he repacked his black bag. "While I advised bed rest, she's bound and determined to play that match this afternoon." He glanced out the window. "If there is a match today," he said, eyeing the water streaming down the window.

"Isn't that dangerous?" Alex asked, concerned about Serena's pallor as she sat in an armchair, wrapped in a blanket.

The doctor shrugged his shoulders. Alex wondered what kind of professional wore an orange windbreaker over a yellow polo shirt. He wished someone more experienced, more established—hell, he admitted, older—had answered the call. This guy didn't look as if he'd begun to shave.

"Foolish, perhaps," the physician answered, giving Serena a pat on the head. Alex knew she was feeling rotten when she didn't automatically bristle at the condescending gesture. "But she's in no danger.

"Good luck, Miss Lawrence," he said over his shoulder as he walked toward the door. "I've got a ten-pound bet on you today." With that parting remark, he was gone.

Alex's dark eyes skimmed her pale face. "You look a lot better," he said encouragingly.

Serena brushed her hair out of her eyes. "Liar." She pushed her palms down on the arms of the chair in an attempt to rise to her feet.

"Good idea." He moved quickly to put his arm around her waist. "Let me help you back into bed, love."

"Bed? I'm not going back to bed. I'm going to take a shower."

Alex stared at her incredulously. "A shower? Serena, you can't even stand up. How do you think you're going to take a shower?"

Good point. "All right. A bath," she decided. "I'll take a bath."

"You're going back to bed," he stated resolutely, moving her in the direction of the double bed.

With a surprising show of strength, Serena shook free of his arm. "I'm going to take a bath," she repeated firmly. "And then I'm going to get dressed."

"And then?" he challenged, dreading the answer he knew was coming.

She lifted her blond head in a gesture befitting the Ice Princess. "And then I'm going to go downstairs, get in the limousine and go play my Wimbledon final." As a sudden attack of vertigo caused her head to swim, Serena blinked furiously to rid herself of the sickening dizziness. "A final I intend to win," she said with a ragged breath.

Alex fought the urge to shake her. She was ill, he re minded himself. Emotionally upset. Understandably over wrought. She had waited more than two years for this day She had dedicated herself to her comeback, overcoming in credible odds. It was only natural that she would be disap pointed. Hell, devastated, he admitted. But she'd get over it There was more to life than tennis. He could make Serena see that now.

"At what cost?" he asked quietly.

She pressed her palm against the door of the bathroom for balance as she looked at him curiously. "Cost?"

"What risks are you willing to take to play this game today?"

As ill as she was, Serena could not miss the scorn Alex placed on the word game. After all this time, she considered, not knowing whether to be furious or hurt, he still didn't understand how much all this meant to her. She had thought that after being with her during the French Open and now Wimbledon, Alex would come to appreciate that, to her, tennis was more than a mere game. More than a pleasant way to pass a Sunday afternoon. It was her life, damn it! Why couldn't he see that?

"I'm not taking any risks, Alex. The doctor assured me that the shot would probably take care of my nausea in twenty or thirty minutes. As for my weakness, I'll just have to overcome it. My father always said—"

"I don't give a damn about what your father said!" Alex roared, suddenly losing patience. "When are you going to grow up and stop trying to win the man's approval? He's dead, Serena. He's been dead for eight years. You don't have to keep killing yourself to meet some ridiculous standard of behavior your father set for you when you were still too young to know any better!"

"It's not ridiculous. My father taught me how to win, Alex. It's because of him that I'm playing in that final today. Don't you understand? Don't you care?"

Anger, resentment, frustration surged through him like molten lava. Alex hadn't realized he had a temper until it had begun building. Hotter and stronger than anything he could have imagined.

"I don't give a damn about William Lawrence. I don't care about serves, volleys, whether clay is better than grass, old players more skilled than new. It might sound like heresy,

Serena, but right now I don't care anything about Wimbledon, Centre Court or any of it. I only care about you!"

"If you really cared about me, you'd understand that I do care about all those things," Serena fired back. "I'm a tennis player."

With an uncharacteristically savage oath, Alex shot his fist in the direction of the wall. Serena gasped as he stopped just in time. Needing something to do with his hands, he shoved them into his pockets so forcefully that the seams broke. Change scattered over the faded rose Aubusson rug underfoot. Neither Serena nor Alex noticed.

"You're a woman first," he said tightly. "A flesh-and-blood woman. A pregnant woman."

Serena stared at him. "Pregnant?"

Alex groaned inwardly as he wondered what had ever happened to the skillful diplomat he had once been. His timing, never mind his method, left a great deal to be desired. If he had been this effective in his former career, the world would have been embroiled in World War Three years ago.

"You don't have to keep it from me any longer, Serena," he said in what he hoped was a conciliatory tone.

He moved toward her, his arms outstretched, but Serena only backed away in response, her eyes wide with obvious shock. Damn. He'd frightened her with his near loss of temper. What on earth had he been thinking of, going off the handle like that?

"Honey, I love you," he soothed. "I've loved you for weeks. For months. I think I fell in love with you the first moment I saw you in the garden. And I'll love our baby."

Serena wondered if she could possibly be delirious. What in heaven's name was he talking about? She pressed her palm experimentally against her stomach, half expecting to discover it swollen with child. *A hallucination*, she assured herself. *That's all this is. Take a deep breath, close your eyes and when you open them, it'll all be gone.*

No such luck. When she opened her wary eyes, Alex was still standing a few feet away, his dark gaze filled with loving reassurance and obvious concern.

"Alex, I'm not pregnant," Serena said softly.

"Of course you are." He reached out and grasped her hand. "It's all right, honey. I've suspected for weeks. I think it's wonderful."

If Serena had not been so shocked by his false assumption, not to mention ill, she might have dwelt a bit longer on the odd mixture of pride and happiness on Alex's face. Unfortunately, her feverish mind could only concentrate on the obvious.

"It's flu," she insisted. "The doctor said so."

"Not that I give a lot of credence to what that British Yuppie had to say, but I'll accept the fact that you may have caught the flu that's going around," Alex allowed. "But I didn't sleep through all my college biology lectures, Serena. And I can count."

God, her head hurt. If only the pounding would stop long enough for her to think straight. "What does that mean?"

"It means that we've been lovers six weeks. Did you think that I wouldn't notice you haven't had a period in all that time?"

"Oh, God," Serena groaned. "If you'd only said something."

Alex felt a cold, ominous hand reaching around his heart. Something wasn't quite right. In fact, something was very, very wrong. "If I had," he said tentatively, "what would you have told me?"

"I'd have told you that this has happened before when I'm under the stress of back-to-back tournaments. I never gave the matter any thought."

Alex dropped Serena's hand to sink down into the chair she had recently vacated. "She didn't give the matter any thought," he mumbled. His expression suddenly brightened. "You still could be pregnant. Nothing you've said so far rules out that possibility. So you have the flu, and the stress has your cycle messed up. You could still be pregnant, Serena."

"I can't," she whispered.

"Of course you can," he argued. "Serena, do you have any idea how many times we've made love since that first night in Washington? It would be amazing if you *weren't* pregnant."

Serena felt like an assassin as she killed the light shining in his eyes. "I'm not pregnant because I'm on the Pill."

The resulting silence was actually audible, screeching around them until Serena wanted to cover her ears to shut it out. Alex's warm, dark eyes, which only moments before had been filled with love, hardened to obsidian, the planes of his face to granite.

"You're on the Pill," he repeated slowly. Serena could practically see the wheels turning inside his head. "But you told me that there wasn't a man in your life during your time in the clinic."

"There wasn't. I went to a doctor before the Washington trip," she said softly.

"Why?"

Serena lifted her shoulders then let them fall. "The answer should be obvious, Alex. You were right all along. It was inevitable that we would become lovers. I could see it getting closer to happening every day."

As her ragged breath filled the room, Alex fought the urge to go to her. To comfort her. Soothe her. She was tearing his heart out, piece by piece, and he couldn't even hate her for it.

Serena's voice was a whisper, but easily heard in the stifling stillness. "I had to protect myself."

"Against me?" he asked incredulously. "I'd never hurt you."

"Not against you. Against having a child." Unable to stand his intense gaze another moment, Serena turned away, staring blindly out at the silver rain lashing against the glass.

With an oddly detached sense of observation, Alex realized that he hadn't known how horribly it hurt to break a heart. He'd broken his nose once, while on the boxing team at Oxford. Or more precisely, his opponent had broken it for him. That incident had taught Alex that he wasn't cut out to be a pugilist. He'd broken his ankle jumping off the roof of his house in Cairo when he was seven. That little episode had proven that umbrellas made lousy parachutes. But until now, until Serena, his heart had managed to escape unscathed. He wondered what the lesson would be this time.

"Foolish of me to have forgotten your feelings about children," he said acidly.

"I like children," Serena argued weakly.

"Other people's children."

Serena swallowed, but her throat remained dry. "Alex, try to understand. There's just no place in my life for a child."

"Because you're too selfish," he exploded, his words lashing at her like a whip. "All you care about is your damn game. Your ranking. Your championships. Your picture in all the papers." His eyes blazed. "You're about as capable of giving love as one of those damn machines that shoots balls all day."

"That's not true." Serena whirled around, her tormented eyes bright with unshed tears. "You don't understand!"

"Oh, I understand, sweetheart." His gaze raked over her, viciously accusing. "I understand that I've been used by an expert." He saw the pain flood into her eyes, viewed her fingers twisting together, but Alex didn't want to consider what she could be feeling. Not while his own hurt was so raw. He turned away and marched toward the door.

Serena held out her hand in an impotent gesture. "Where are you going?"

"Back to Claremont. Where I belong."

"But I love you," she cried passionately. It had not been how she had planned to tell him. But she couldn't let him leave without the words being said. "I need you." Desperation caused her to push the admission past the lump in her throat.

Steeped in his own anguish, Alex chose to misinterpret Serena's words. "That shouldn't be any problem," he ground out. "Next time you're feeling romantic, princess, try taking your tennis racket to bed!"

Serena stared as the door slammed behind him. Then she covered her face with her hands and cried.

"THIS IS, WITHOUT A DOUBT, the dumbest thing I've ever heard of," Donovan ground out as he paced the floor of Serena's hotel room.

Serena listlessly dragged the brush through her hair. "I don't have any choice," she said, as she met Donovan's frustrated gaze in the mirror.

"I agree with your brother." Marty Jennings was sprawled in the chair, watching Serena's attempt to get ready. "Let me call and notify them that you're going to default," he insisted, not for the first time since arriving to find Serena looking like death warmed over.

"No one defaults on a Wimbledon final. The day my father won his fifth Wimbledon championship, he went straight from Centre Court to the hospital."

"Where he was operated on for appendicitis," Marty added dryly. "I've heard that story, Serena. We've all heard that story. And just because William Lawrence was a damn fool doesn't mean you have to follow in his footsteps."

"My father was a champion," she said, returning the brush to the dressing table with a sigh of relief. The doctor had been right about the injection stopping her nausea, but she felt so weak.

"Look at you," Donovan argued. "You can't even lift that damn brush. How do you expect to swing a racket?"

"I'll manage."

Marty was on his feet, standing over her. "Sweetheart, it's time you faced the truth. William Lawrence was a self-centered bastard whose entire life revolved around the game of tennis because he was too emotionally bereft to feel anything for anyone."

Scarlet flags waved in Serena's cheeks in direct contrast to the snowy pallor of her complexion. "My father loved me," she protested.

"He loved what you could be," Marty corrected firmly. He knelt down, his fingers cupped on her shoulders. "Serena, honey, I knew the man. If you hadn't been born with an incredible talent, he wouldn't have noticed you were alive."

"He loved me," she repeated raggedly.

"He loved playing God."

As if he could read her mind, as if he knew the self-recriminations that were racing through it at this moment, the older man took both her icy hands in his. "Serena, I love you. Your brother loves you. And unless my eyes have gone from old age, that fella who's been tagging after you like a lovesick cocker spaniel for the past six weeks loves you.

"Your father's attitude didn't have anything to do with you. It was just the way he was. William Lawrence was admittedly a brilliant tennis player. One of the all-time great champions. But that's all he was. It was all he could ever be."

All he could ever be. Wasn't that all she had ever been, Serena asked herself. Being Serena Lawrence, tennis champion, had been a twenty-four-hour-a-day job. From the time she was five years old. Twenty-three years, Serena thought sadly. Twenty-three years she could never recover. Alex had been right. She had been living a one-dimensional life until he had come along and turned her world upside down. And now he was gone. She groaned.

"See," Donovan pointed out, "you're sick, babe. Let's call it a day. There's always next year."

"No." She rose shakily to her feet. "I'm going to play. I might not win, but those people who have been standing in the rain all morning have paid to see me. And I'm going to give them the best show I can."

Both men shrugged helplessly as she plucked her violet warm-up jacket from the coatrack. "Gentlemen?"

The hotel lobby swarmed with players. Those who had not yet been eliminated were wearing warm-up suits as they waited for rides to the Queen's Club where, if the rain let up, practice sessions would be held. Others, for whom the tournament had ended prematurely, were waiting to be driven to the All-England Club itself to witness the women's finals. Several called out wishes of good luck as Serena made her way shakily through the crowd.

"Wait a minute," she said abruptly as they reached the revolving door. She shook free of Donovan's hand and turned back toward the bank of elevators.

"Now what?" her brother asked on an exasperated breath.

"I forgot something upstairs."

"I'll get it," Donovan offered.

"You'll never find it," Serena hedged. "I can't remember exactly where I put it." Before either man could offer another word of objection, she was headed back across the lobby.

Once in her room, Serena reached under her pillow, taking out a worn copper coin. When Alex had first given it to her, after their picnic at Kensington Gardens, Serena had been skeptical of its powers. William Lawrence's daughter was far too levelheaded to believe in magic. Her father had seen to that. Yet some teasing little urge had encouraged her to slip it into her pocket the following day.

After winning that match in straight sets, Serena had decided that, although she wasn't the slightest bit superstitious, just knowing that the coin was in her pocket made her feel a little more confident. And now, with her personal life lying in ruins, it helped Serena feel as if Alex was with her. At least in spirit.

"Ready," she said with a smile that wavered only slightly
as she rejoined her brother and her coach. "Let's get this show
on the road."

It was an hour's ride from her hotel, around the corner
from Big Ben, to the All-England Lawn Tennis and Croquet
Club. The limousine crossed the Thames then wove its way
through the traffic maze of south London. When it pulled
through the black iron Doherty Gates, Serena's heart beat a
great deal faster.

The players' waiting room was abloom with fresh flowers.
A couch, two wicker chairs and a cheval mirror constituted
the furnishings, along with a television set where waiting
players could watch the match currently being played. At this
moment, there was nothing to watch. All the courts had been
covered in deference to the rain, and the starting time of two
o'clock had already been moved to three. Then four. Finally
the committee decided to attempt to begin the match at six
o'clock. Serena had been waiting over six hours.

The doctor had arrived with another injection, which settled her stomach but left her feeling slightly disoriented. That
sensation was not helped by the fact that her rebellious mind
kept rerunning that final scene with Alex. Over and over
again, until she thought she'd scream. For the first three hours
she had looked up from where she was lying on the floral
couch each time the door opened, hoping against hope that
Alex would walk across the threshold. But each time Serena
was disappointed.

Several times during the day, she sent Donovan to ring
Alex's hotel room. But time after time the telephone went
unanswered. When the official popped his head in to tell
Serena that she was expected on Centre Court in ten minutes, she gave up on finding him. It was time to think about
why she was here. She knew that back in North Carolina the
patients at the clinic would be rooting for her, as if her suc-

cess was a portent of things to come for the rest of them. They would understand if she failed to win, but she owed it to all of them to play her best. And she couldn't do that if her mind wasn't on her game.

As she entered Center Court, carrying the traditional bouquet, Serena said a silent prayer that Alex would be seated in his customary spot in the friends' box. When he wasn't there, her heart sank to the damp grass underfoot. Handing the sterling-silver roses to a ball girl, she took her place in the backcourt. Her opponent, Kathy Fleming, won the racket spin for first service.

Centre Court was more than the grass playing field; it was like a theater, with one tennis court being the stage. And at this moment, more than twenty-nine thousand pairs of eyes were directed toward the drama about to be played.

To her dismay, Serena soon discovered that the match was as much a battle against herself as it was against her opponent. Despite the fact that William Lawrence had drummed the need to concentrate into Serena from the time her head had barely come to the top of the net, she was allowing uninvited thoughts to surface. Alex. Her mind created demons, impish little monsters born of her own folly who whispered words of melancholy into her ears.

The crowd quickly sensed Serena's despair. When the word had leaked out that the doctor had visited her hotel room this morning, the headlines on Fleet Street had predicted a rout. Bookmakers had scrambled to keep up with the bets pouring in, the odds on Serena plummeting as the day progressed. By the time the match had begun, Serena, who had climbed through the ranks to become a 2-1 favorite the day before, was a 10-1 underdog.

Displaying their national favoritism for underdogs, the predominantly British crowd began to urge her on. While the verbal encouragement remained undeniably restrained for the usually polite Wimbledon fans, the shouts and groans resembled pandemonium. When Serena double-faulted in the first set, already down two games, the moans brought to mind a Greek chorus of doomsters.

Despite her illness—her head was spinning and her legs had turned to water—Serena knew that her problem was more mental than physical. Her situation with Alex sat next to her during changeovers; it whispered to her at the baseline and nagged her at the net. As the pressure increased, she became tighter, her strokes shorter and more rigid, her shots far less penetrating.

It began to rain again, light sprinkles that made the grass as slick as ice. Serena fell more than once on the slippery surface, her snowy-white skirt streaked with angry green stains. The rain intensified, dime-size drops streaking down her cheeks, pounding on the top of her head. Fleming moved in for the kill, blasting the ball over the net.

The ball tore past Serena with the speed of sound. Refusing to give up, she dove for it and slipped, dropping her racket as she sprawled onto the spongy wet surface. As she rose wearily to her knees, Serena felt a glow of warmth come over her, like a warm, comforting quilt. Her eyes cut immediately to the friends' box where her gaze locked with Alex's. As he gave her the familiar thumbs-up sign, Serena pushed herself the rest of the way to her feet. She might be down 5-1, but she was a long way from out.

As the crowd roared its approval, Serena fought back, winning enough points to take the next game. The score in the first set was now 5-2 and the Wimbledon fans, in an unprecedented show of support, were on their feet.

Though Serena had made a valiant return, she soon found herself down set point. Fleming, her own pristine white tennis dress beginning to bear grass stains, let loose a blistering serve that gave Serena no opportunity to get a racket on it. With that ace, Fleming took the first set 6-2.

Despite the rain streaming down her face, despite the stinging grass burn on her right knee, despite her lingering headache, Serena began to feel she might have an opportunity to pull the match out. She paced the backcourt, trying to walk off the stiffness in her knee. The dampness was not helping her arm, but she had played with worse.

Before they could begin the second set, the officials, who had been gathered in a huddle on the sidelines, went over to talk to the umpire, who nodded his head in agreement. It was growing dark and the rain was slanting harder. To no one's surprise, except perhaps the two combatants', who had been concentrating on the game, the match was stopped. The fans immediately returned to their characteristic docile behavior. No one objected. They simply opened their umbrellas and filed peaceably from the grandstand.

The two women exchanged a long look, then walked to the sidelines. They'd meet again tomorrow.

Serena found herself immediately wrapped in a warm blanket. "You came," she said breathlessly, looking up at Alex. Tears mingled with the raindrops captured in her dark lashes.

"Of course," he said simply.

"We need to talk. I've been thinking about what you said."

He pressed his lips against her hair. "Later. First we have to get you back to bed."

She tilted her head back to give him a watery smile. "What a wonderful suggestion."

Alex gave her a quick, hard hug. He knew their problems were a long way from being solved. But he loved her. More than he ever would have thought it possible to love anyone. At this moment, that was all that mattered.

He flashed her a brilliantly rewarding smile. "You *are* feeling better," he said as he walked her toward the dressing room while Donovan and Marty ran interference in front of them, keeping the reporters at bay.

"I DIDN'T KNOW if you'd be back," Serena admitted later.

She had willingly accepted the luxury of a long, hot bath, a light meal from room service and the pampering that Alex insisted on giving. Now she was propped up in bed, newly fluffed pillows behind her back. She was beginning to feel much better, she decided as she rubbed Alex's copper talisman between her fingers. With any luck, the flu would run its course, tomorrow would dawn bright and sunny and she'd get a second chance to take home the championship. Now if only he'd stop the incessant pacing. It was driving her up a wall.

"You should have known," Alex said as he stared out into the well of darkness outside the rain-streaked window. "If I had handled things right from the beginning, you never would have doubted me."

Serena stared at his rigid back. If *he* had handled things? "It was my fault." She brushed at her bangs with a hand that was none too steady. "I should have told you about the Pill from the beginning. I should have explained about my mother and my father. And their marriage, and my tennis and . . ."

Her voice drifted off as she buried her face in her hands. "You were right," she murmured. "I'm a washout at being a woman."

Alex was beside her in two long strides, sitting on the edge of the bed, wrapping her in the security of his embrace. "I'm the one who screwed things up," he corrected harshly. "I thought I had everything under control. Hell, after handling tensions in the Middle East without batting an eye, I figured a romance would be a cakewalk." He smiled down at her. "I was wrong."

Serena pressed her hand against his cheek. "I have so much I want to say to you."

Turning his head, he kissed the soft skin of her palm. "Tomorrow."

Serena shook her head, pleased when it didn't feel in danger of splitting in two. "But—"

"Tomorrow," Alex interjected strongly. His hands smoothed her shoulders. "You've had a rough day. You're not well, and I didn't help matters by having a temper tantrum a five-year-old would have envied. I had a lot of time to think while I was walking around London in the rain today. And while I hate to admit to being less than perfect, it occurred to me that I've been insisting on having things all my way from the beginning."

As Serena opened her mouth to argue, Alex held up a hand. "I was walking along Jerymn Street when I caught a glimpse of my reflection in the window of a cheesemonger's shop. Do you know what I saw?"

Serena shook her head.

"A very selfish man staring back at me." His lips quirked slightly under his mustache. "Oh, he was handsome enough, and even a little debonair, if I may say so." He waited for Serena's nod of agreement. "However, he was the most presumptuous bastard God ever put on this green earth."

Alex's hand caressed her arm almost absently as he struggled to remember his carefully rehearsed speech. Her nearness, her warmth, the soft, feminine scent drifting upward from her hair conspired to expunge the words from his mind. *Don't let me mess this up*, he begged whatever unseen force had been controlling their lives.

"I love you, Serena Lawrence. I wasn't expecting it to happen; in fact, to tell you the truth, when I realized precisely why you had been driving me crazy, I wasn't sure the answer made me very happy. I had always considered my life pleasant. Enjoyable. Convenient. The women I knew didn't want commitment any more than I did."

Had he ever made a lengthier speech? Probably not, Alex decided. But he'd never made a more important one, either. He took a deep breath.

"Then I fell in love with you and discovered I wanted commitments. Strings. A long, luxurious lifetime of strings. I wanted to marry you. I wanted us to live in a house with a white picket fence, two point five kids and a big dog who'd insist on burying his bones in the rose garden. Everything I'd always secretly laughed at suddenly looked like the gold at the end of the rainbow. I was so wrapped up in myself that I never considered the fact that what I thought of as bonds of love you might view as shackles.

"I still want to marry you, Serena. I still want that family. And I'm going to do my damnedest to make you want those things, too. But in the meantime, I'll take whatever it is you're prepared to offer."

Serena stared at him for a full, long minute. His voice had been rough with the emotion still burning in his eyes. It was a frightening feeling to be so loved. So wanted. As her bottom lip began to quiver, Serena bit down. Hard.

"I never knew," she whispered.

"Now you do," Alex said simply. He gave her an encouraging smile. "You were right, we do have to talk. But let's get the last two sets of that final under your belt before we sit down at the negotiation table."

"If you insist," Serena said with a soft sigh. She'd heard that tone before. Whenever he refused to take no for an answer. "But I want to say just one thing."

"One thing," he agreed, wondering if life with Serena was going to be one continuing bargaining session. Considering the alternative, Alex decided he could do a great deal worse.

"I do so love you," she said soberly, her gray eyes more serious than he had ever seen them.

His thumb brushed her lower lip, caressing the place her teeth had worried her tender skin. So soft, he thought. So lovely. But strong. Serena was everything a man could ever want in a woman. She was more than he could have imagined in his most fanciful daydreams. And like a fool, he had almost thrown what they had away.

"You should get some sleep."

She pressed her palms against his chest. "I have a better idea."

His heart trebled its beat. "But you're sick."

Serena unbuttoned a single button on his blue oxford-cloth shirt, allowing her fingers to slip through the opening where they played with his crisp dark chest hair. "I'm feeling much better," she wheedled prettily. Two more buttons followed. Alex groaned as she pressed her lips against the warm, male fragrant skin of his chest.

"Serena," he warned with a ragged thread of sound.

"Yes, my darling?" She continued to unbutton his shirt, her lips following the path her fingers had forged.

"Are you by any chance trying to seduce me?"

Her eyes as they lifted to his sparkled attractively. "That's one of the things I've always loved about you, Alex," she said throatily as she pulled the shirt loose from his slacks. Her fingers played with the buckle of his belt. "You're so very observant."

He covered her hands with his. "I'll make you a deal."

Just the sight of his gleaming chest made her bones melt. Serena was grateful she was lying down. "I'm always willing to listen."

As her fingers slipped past his waistband, fire skimmed through his veins. "I can't think of anything I'd rather do than make love to you."

Her teeth nipped at the cord in his neck. "Why do I hear a *but* in that lovely declaration?"

Alex fought against the need as it curled through him. "No buts," he ground out, stifling the groan that rose from the depths of his chest as her hand trailed up his thigh, her fingernails scraping on the denim of the jeans he'd changed into after arriving back at the room. "However, in deference to your condition, I insist on doing all the work."

Serena's smile reminded him of the one Eve probably flashed at Adam while tempting him with that shiny red apple. She lay back against the pillow, her eyes gleaming with expectant lights.

"Why, Mr. Bedare," she crooned, "I do believe that's the most diplomatic suggestion you've come up with yet."

He ducked his head and pressed his lips against hers. There was nothing tentative about the kiss. His mouth drank from hers as if he had just survived a trek across the blazing Sahara. His tongue swept the sensitive interior like fingers of flame, setting her skin on fire and scorching her mind. The dizziness she had experienced this morning was nothing compared to what she was feeling now.

She took his hands and pressed them against her breasts. "I need you," she said softly, all laughter dissolving as his touch burned through the emerald satin of her nightgown.

Closing her eyes to his beguiling touch, Serena felt her nightgown drift away, allowing his hands increasing intimacies. Where he led, she followed willingly, letting him bring her to higher and higher planes of desire. Only the soft little moans that escaped her parted lips and the rapid beat of her heart under his mouth revealed her rising passion.

"You're mine," he growled possessively as he pressed his palm against the dampening warmth of her.

"Yes," Serena said on a gasp that was part pleasure, part pain. "Oh, yes."

No longer passive, she moved under him, her hands fretting across his back, his thighs, the firm flesh of his buttocks. Her whispered words of love were unintelligible as she rained kisses over his face. She was breathing hard as she broke the heated contact and opened her eyes to stare deep into the swirling ebony depths only inches away. Her legs wrapped around his thighs as she lifted her hips in silent invitation.

"Now," she said achingly.

"Now," Alex agreed. *Forever.*

Then there was only howling winds and bolts of phosphorous lightning. Flashes of blinding light, crashes of thunder. Speed. Heat. Caught in a speeding whirlwind of flame, they clung to each other, drawn into a seemingly endless vortex of dark desire, pulled deeper and deeper still, until the world finally shattered into shards of crystalline brilliance and they emerged safely on the other side.

THE LATE-MORNING SUNSHINE gilded the windowpanes of the Players' Tea Room. The large bay windows faced the scoreboard, which listed who was playing on every court. Serena's had not been the only match canceled yesterday and the room was filled with players waiting to resume their part in the tournaments. Harried officials clad in dark blazers and gray flannel slacks looked as if they had been awake all night, as indeed they had. Outside fans were milling around in the walkways, hoping for a glimpse of someone famous. The tension in the air was palpable, but Serena had never felt more at ease.

She had gone to sleep envisioning what she was going to do today. Point after point had been examined, dissected and planned for. Including the euphoria of winning. Her headache was gone; her stomach had accepted a light breakfast.

She smiled as she glanced around the room, breathing in the scent of fresh-cut flowers in Waterford vases. The room, a jumble of glass tables and white-wicker chairs, was abloom with blazing colors. Kathy Fleming was seated a few feet away, basking in the glow of expected victory. Her eyes, when they slid from time to time to Serena, blazed with triumphant lights.

"It's not over till it's over," Serena murmured, as much to herself as to Alex, who sat beside her.

"That's baseball," he pointed out. "Yogi Berra."

Serena shrugged. "Same thing."

There was laughter from the other table. "She's definitely not suffering from a lack of self-confidence," Alex ground out.

Serena smiled at his irritated expression. She slipped her hand into his. "That could work to my advantage," she said without rancor. "Besides, she's still young. She's got a lot to learn."

"Twenty-eight is so old?"

"Middle-aged, for a tennis pro," she decided after giving the matter some thought. "Do you know while I was waiting for the rain to let up yesterday, I realized that I've been a professional tennis player for half my life."

"It's been a good life, hasn't it?"

Those long lonely hours had given her plenty of time to think and Serena was ready with her answer. "For the most part. Yet whenever people asked me when I was going to quit, I never had an answer for them. Because I couldn't contemplate a life outside of tennis."

Alex could hear the emotion welling up in her voice and squeezed her fingers affectionately. "We were going to wait until later for this discussion," he reminded her.

Serena sighed as she stretched her legs out and looked down at her shoes. She had been averaging a pair of tennis shoes a week for the past fourteen years. It was rather depressing to realize that her life could be represented by seven hundred and twenty-eight pairs of tennis shoes and shelves and trunks filled with silver trophies.

"Later," she agreed. As she rose to her feet, her hands were ice cold.

"Are you having another chill?" Alex asked, immediately concerned.

"Prematch jitters," Serena admitted with a wry smile. At his worried look she brushed a quick kiss against his tight lips. "Keeps me on my toes," she assured him.

His love blazed in his dark eyes. "Good luck."

Serena dug into the pocket of her skirt. "Can't miss," she said, flipping the copper coin in the air. "I think we've got this little guy to thank for all the rain yesterday."

"For more than that," Alex said, deciding that the first thing he was going to do after Serena's match was to send Carly flowers. He wondered idly how many dozen roses would even come close to professing his appreciation.

They exchanged a long look. "For more than that," Serena agreed softly.

THE WIND WAS SWIRLING everywhere inside Centre Court, but Serena barely noticed. As she had suspected, Fleming's overconfidence worked to Serena's advantage. At first Serena concentrated on her percentage shots. She hit an approach shot down the line. Forced to dive for the ball, Fleming barely blooped it over the net where Serena returned it crosscourt.

Her instincts took over as she forgot to worry about hitting the ball. It was as if Serena overlooked the fact that her opponent was across the net, appreciating her only in an abstract, detached way as she transported herself beyond the turmoil of the match to some place of total peace and calm. Her ground strokes became weapons; she produced passing shots with uncanny efficiency. She hit winners when she was out of position and found angles most players would not have guessed existed.

By the time Fleming realized that she was in trouble, that she was not being given the chance to hit the big balls she had the previous day, Serena was on a roll that everyone watching knew was going to be difficult, if not impossible, to stop. Serena's experience proved a decided edge as Fleming tried to go for too much with her shots, falling into a trap that she couldn't escape. When she hit a backhand into the net to give Serena the match, there was a moment of stunned silence. Then deafening applause.

In a display of emotion the Ice Princess would rather have died than allow, Serena threw her racket into the air. Then she ran to the net to give her opponent a conciliatory hug. Kathy Fleming, still stunned by Serena's amazing comeback, appeared to appreciate the gesture.

Serena was barely aware of the carpet being rolled out from the Royal Box where the ceremonies were to be held. She did remember to curtsy as she received her silver salver, but she had no idea what she said into the microphones being thrust in front of her as she made her way toward the three men who were waiting for her.

Alex stood back, motioning Donovan and Marty forward for their embraces first. He was going to have her to himself all night. Every night. He could afford to be generous.

Serena's smile was beatific as she finally flung her arms around Alex's neck. "First we talk," she murmured in his ear as he lifted her off her feet. "Then do I have plans for you."

His laughing eyes skimmed her white dress, which today didn't possess so much as a wrinkle. "Don't you want to change first?"

"I just want to get out of here," she said, handing the silver tray to Donovan. "I want to be alone with you."

Alex wasn't going to wait for Serena to ask twice. Putting his arm around her, he attempted to maneuver her through the crowd to where the limousine was waiting. It was not an easy task. Someone plunked a baby into her arms, she was handed programs, hats, ice-cream wrappers to autograph. Fans pulled at her sweater, as if trying to steal some little part of her fame.

Finally, they were in each other's arms in the wide back seat as the long black car wound its way back toward London.

"What kind of carpenter are you?" Serena asked after a long, lingering kiss. She was wrapped in his arms, her head leaning back against his shoulders.

Alex was playing with her hair, twisting the silken blond strands around his fingers. "I've been known to smash my thumb if I get within twenty feet of a hammer," he answered absently as he pressed his lips against the top of her head. Sweet. She smelled so sweet. "Why?"

"That's all right," she assured him. "We'll just have to hire a carpenter."

Alex found Serena's smile as stunning and provocative as everything else about her. *Pixilated*, he realized. That's what he was. "A carpenter?"

She patted his cheek. Alex was a dear. And certainly one of the most intelligent men she had ever met. But he could be so vague at times that he almost reminded her of Donovan.

"For the picket fence, of course," she reminded him patiently. "And I'm sure we can find the perfect dog at the Claremont animal shelter. We'll request one who likes to bury bones." Wrinkles gathered in her smooth brow. "As for the children, Alex, I'm afraid I'm going to have to request some cooperation."

"Children?"

He knew he was sounding like a damn parrot, repeating everything she said. But her total capitulation was coming as a shock. The most he had hoped for was that Serena would agree to live together. One day at a time.

"Children," she repeated. "I can't promise you a basketball team like your friend, Patrick, but the dog will need someone to play with. What would you say to a boy and a girl?"

Alex was suddenly very still. "Are you sure you aren't just high from winning the match?"

"Well, of course I'm high," Serena countered. "In fact, I'm floating on air and I have absolutely no intention of coming down for at least a week. But that has nothing to do with my decision. I made my mind up yesterday."

"Yesterday," Alex echoed. And to think he'd lain awake all night, watching Serena sleep, terrified of what her answer might be.

She nodded decisively. "Yesterday." Her soft eyes gleamed silver in the sunlight.

"What about your tennis?" he had to ask, dreading the answer.

"Oh, that." Serena leaned back against him, putting her feet up on the seat. "I figured that we could get married right away. Tomorrow if possible." She glanced up at him. "I don't want to rush you, Alex, but I would like to do it before Donovan returns to Gloria."

"Tomorrow's fine," he agreed weakly.

Serena smiled. "Good. Then I thought we could honey-moon in Europe during your semester break."

His hands moved up and down her arms. "You're on a roll. What about after the honeymoon?"

Her gaze was teasingly censorious. "What makes you think it's going to end?"

He kissed her. "I stand corrected. What are we going to do when we tire of traveling?"

"Well, first there's Forest Hills. Then, of course, we should schedule a trip to Washington before returning to Clare-mont. I'm assuming you'd like to be there when your friend has her baby."

Stunned by the thought Serena had given to every detail, Alex could only nod.

She reached up to run her fingers through his hair. "The Australian Open is during your Thanksgiving break. I called the college while you were taking your shower this morning and checked on the dates," she explained when she saw his incredulous expression.

"So anyway, I figured that you could come to Melbourne and watch me make it a grand slam. Then, with any luck, and a lot of sacrifice and hard work on your part, darling, we should be able to get me pregnant by Christmas." She grinned up at him. "You won't mind if I keep that penny a little longer, will you?"

"It's yours," he said promptly. "Am I allowed to ask if you're going to continue to play professionally?"

"Probably," Serena said thoughtfully. "Although nothing like I have in the past. I'll only play in tournaments that are scheduled during your breaks." She traced his smiling lips with her finger. "They say travel is very broadening for chil-dren."

"You've got it all figured out, haven't you?" Alex asked wonderingly.

The smile slowly faded from Serena's face. "Do you mind?"

"What do you think?"

Serena put her hand on the back of his dark head, drawing his lips down to hers. "I think, my darling," she murmured, punctuating her words with soft, tantalizing kisses, "that this could be the start of a beautiful friendship."

**The lucky penny continues to
bring good fortune and romance in . . .**

Tempting Fate

Professor Donavan Kincaid didn't believe
in fate, but Brooke Stirling's return to
Smiley College *had* to be more than
coincidence. Twelve years earlier they'd
been fellow students—and lovers—until
he'd broken Brooke's heart. Now, with the
magic penny in hand, Donovan was
determined to resurrect the love and
passion they'd once shared. . . .

#153 *Tempting Fate* is the final book in a
sizzling trilogy by best-selling author
JoAnn Ross. The series began with #126
Magic in the Night, followed by #137
Playing for Keeps. Look for *Tempting Fate*
in May 1987!

Harlequin Temptation

COMING NEXT MONTH

#141 LOVE IN TANDEM Lynda Ward

When Meredith first ran into Brandt, they were both stunned by the impact. Of course, she *had* knocked him off his bicycle. But what happened between them later was no accident....

#142 NO PASSING FANCY Mary Jo Territo

O'Mara was a man with fantastic moves, but Jo was the woman to show him a thing or two more....

#143 BED AND BREAKFAST Kate McKenzie

When Leslie O'Neill moved into the quaint but chaotic Seaview Inn, she suspected her stay would be less than serene. Already she was wishing her charming host, Greg Austin, would offer her more than bed and breakfast....

#144 TWELVE ACROSS Barbara Delinsky

Leah hadn't planned on being stranded in Garrick's secluded cabin. But she had no more control over the storm outside than the one that raged within.

What readers say about Harlequin Temptation . . .

One word is needed to describe the series Harlequin Temptation . . . "Exquisite." They are so sensual, passionate and beautifully written.

—H.D., Easton, PA

I'm always looking forward to the next month's Harlequin Temptation with a great deal of anticipation . . .

—M.B., Amarillo, TX

I'm so glad you now have Harlequin Temptation . . . the stories seem so real. They really stimulate my imagination!

—S.E.B., El Paso, TX

Names available on request.